STORMSTRUCK

OTHER BOOKS BY CATHY BEVERIDGE

Offside (Thistledown Press, 2001)

Shadows of Disaster (Ronsdale Press, 2003)

Chaos in Halifax (Ronsdale Press, 2004)

One on One (Thistledown Press, 2005)

Stormstruck

Cathy Beveridge

RONSDALE PRESS

STORMSTRUCK
Copyright © 2006 Cathy Beveridge

RONSDALE PRESS
3350 West 21st Avenue, Vancouver, B.C., Canada V6S 1G7
www.ronsdalepress.com

Typesetting: Julie Cochrane, in Minion 12 pt on 16
Front Cover Art: Ljuba Levstek
Cover Design: Julie Cochrane
Paper: Ancient Forest Friendly Rolland "Enviro" — 100% post-consumer
  waste, totally chlorine-free and acid-free

Ronsdale Press wishes to thank the Canada Council for the Arts, the Government of Canada through the Book Publishing Industry Development Program (BPIDP), and the Province of British Columbia through the British Columbia Arts Council for their support of its publishing program.

Library and Archives Canada Cataloguing in Publication

Beveridge, Cathy
  Stormstruck / Cathy Beveridge.

  ISBN-13: 978-1-55380-041-5
  ISBN-10: 1-55380-041-9

  I. Title.

PS8553.E897S86 2006   jC813'.6   C2006-903687-X

Printed in Canada by Marquis Printing, Quebec

for Julie, Michelle and Allison,
may your passion and
determination enable you to
weather life's storms

ACKNOWLEDGEMENTS

I would like to thank Mr. Mac Campbell for his willingness to share his immense historical knowledge of the Goderich area, and for his assistance in ensuring historical accuracy in this novel. I would like also to acknowledge the kindness of Jan Hawley, who extended an invitation to attend the Marine Heritage Festival, where I had the privilege of hearing Mr. Dennis Hale recount his experience as the sole survivor of the *Daniel J. Morrell.* Thanks also to the curators and staff of the Huron and Bruce County Museums who were most helpful. Every attempt has been made to preserve the historical accuracy of the events surrounding the Great Storm of 1913. All characters, however, are entirely fictional.

Chapter one

The highway, like the tail of a fat grey lizard, stretches before Jolene. Waves of heat dance above the hot asphalt. Gingerly, she places one foot in front of the other, following the solid, white centre line. Far ahead, on the horizon, the line and road merge. Jolene slows. She glances over her shoulder, searching for her twin brother Michael, her father, mother and grandfather, but they are absent. The road belongs to her alone and yet she wishes it didn't. Its silent greyness disturbs her. Jolene resumes walking, aware of the odd sensation within her body. It is as if she is made of glass, as if she might shatter. She peers at the horizon. Is that her destination? Does she have the strength to reach it? Does she want to? The questions nag

at her in chants and whispers, filling the space she occupies —
the space between dreaming and waking.

Jolene's eyes blinked open, her dream highway transforming itself into the ceiling panels of the recreational vehicle that she had called home for the past five days. Beside her, Chaos, her ginger-coloured kitten, snuggled closer, his white paws illuminated by a sliver of morning that pierced the RV's skydome. Jolene was grateful for his presence. The dream, which had come three times since they'd left Calgary, always left her feeling edgy.

Michael murmured in his sleep and Jolene looked down from her loft bed into the living area where her brother and grandfather slept. At the far end of the RV, she could hear movements behind her parents' bedroom door. It must be her father. Her mother had stayed behind in Calgary to work with a graduate student at the university. She would join them in a few weeks.

Jolene wondered where they would be then. A month ago that question would not have entered her mind. But that was before Dad had decided to take a family trip across Canada to conduct research for his Museum of Disasters. That was before she and Michael had agreed to relinquish their sports to travel. That was before arrangements had been made with their school to start their grade seven courses on the road. That was before they had followed the Trans-Canada highway, winding its way from the snow-blanketed mountains, across the ironed prairies, over the Canadian Shield to the shores of Lake Huron.

The highway in Jolene's dream was different from the Trans-Canada. No barbed wire fences, gravelled ditches or muddy sloughs edged its shoulders. No semi-trailers, motorcycles, or vehicles rolled over it. She walked it — alone, towards an unknown destination. She wondered why none of her family was in her dream.

Grandpa was awake. His dark green eyes, so like Michael's and her own, were open. He was, she knew, silently composing and rehearsing the stories he would share as the museum's official storyteller. The bedroom door opened with a hushed click and Jolene's father emerged. Grandpa sat up, Chaos yawned, Michael shielded his eyes against the light and Jolene propped herself up on one elbow.

"Well, it looks like everyone's up," said Dad, pulling the blinds open.

"It's already nine o'clock Ontario time," Grandpa informed them.

"Goderich, Ontario, here I come." Dad's voice held the excitement of a child's on Christmas morning. The town of Goderich on Lake Huron's east side would serve as the base for his investigation of the Great Storm of 1913, the worst storm ever to hit the Great Lakes.

"What are your plans, Doug?" asked Grandpa, rising.

"I've got a meeting at the Huron County Museum at ten o'clock. How about you?" The coffee pot gurgled and sputtered.

"I'd like to go to the . . ."

"Library," finished Michael knowingly. Jolene could have

done the same. Libraries, rich in historical collections, were one of Grandpa's favourite places.

"I want to go to the pool," said Michael, throwing back his covers. "Hopefully Goderich has a speed-swimming team I can train with while we're here."

"Good idea," said Dad. "Any plans, Jolene?"

It was a simple, innocent question, but it made her want to shrink beneath her covers and disappear. "No, none." The tone of her words betrayed her agitation. "I have to finish up my science project," she added feebly.

"Okay, but how about coming uptown with the rest of us first and then working on it later this afternoon?" suggested Dad, turning his attention to breakfast.

"No thanks." Jolene pulled her feet upwards, smoothing her sheets and quilt with an unsteady hand. The feeling of fragility that had been present in her dream had returned. She felt as breakable as the eggshells that Dad cracked against the side of his bowl. Yet she wasn't sure why. She and her family were safe in the picturesque town of Goderich. She recalled their drive among the beautiful old stone and brick buildings last night. Dad had found a secluded campsite in a quiet RV resort near the harbour and the Maitland River. Jolene climbed down from the loft bed into a stream of sunshine and set Chaos on the couch. There was no reason to feel out of sorts and yet she did. Michael eyed her curiously, as if her feelings were transparent.

"You can come to the pool with me," he offered.

Jolene did not respond. She brushed past her brother, pulled the cupboard door open with more force than necessary and sorted through the fabrics of her clothes.

"Or you can come to the library," said Grandpa, twirling the ends of his moustache.

"No thanks." She wished they would stop. With each invitation, she felt the cracks within her deepen and widen.

"Do you want to see if there's a gymnastics club in town?" asked Dad.

"That's okay." Jolene chose a shirt from the cupboard and shorts from the neat piles of colours in her drawers and escaped into the tiny bathroom to change. She had already decided not to re-enroll in gymnastics this year, a sport she had been devoted to for the past five years. She'd been spared having to tell her parents when Dad had announced their road trip. Dressed, Jolene stepped back into the living room. "I'm going to take Chaos out," she announced, anxious to be away from her family's good intentions.

A whimsical breeze blew off the water causing a canopy of green leaves above her to tremble, and buoys to clang in the distance. Chaos skittered left, then right, chasing a shimmering blue moth and making Jolene wish she were a cat.

"What a perfect day," said Grandpa, joining her outside with his coffee cup in hand. Chaos somersaulted across the grass, landing face first in a mauve petunia. "Are you sure there isn't anything special you'd like to do today, Jo?"

"There's nothing, Gramps." Didn't he realize that was the

terrible truth? Didn't he understand that was the problem itself? There was nothing special that appealed to her. Nothing that made her leap out of bed or grin like a small child. Nothing that inspired her to feel passionate and alive. Grandpa put an arm around her shoulders and Jolene felt as if she would shatter beneath his touch. Michael had his swimming, Dad had his museum, Grandpa had his stories and history and she . . . she had nothing. She pulled away from her grandfather. "I really want to finish my science project."

Grandpa gave her an unconvinced smile. "All right then. Breakfast is almost ready."

"Thanks, but I'm not hungry."

After her grandfather had gone inside, Jolene watched Chaos torment a ladybug before being distracted by the rapid drumming of a woodpecker. The kitten's antics lightened her spirits and by the time the others stood straddling their bicycles, Jolene was able to manage a reassuring smile. But as she watched them pedal toward the steep incline of North Harbour Road, which would lead them to the town's centre, she scooped up Chaos and hugged him tightly.

Despite what she had told her grandfather, she was in no mood to do her science project. Restless, she deposited the kitten inside the RV and headed for the dirt trail that she and Michael had discovered yesterday evening. Three small cabins, surrounded by the smiling faces of pansies, squatted opposite the small resort pool. Behind them, the Maitland River trickled towards the harbour.

A man with a dirty baseball cap and a belly that protruded over his carpenter's apron pushed a wheelbarrow towards her. He greeted her with a lopsided smile. "You must be Jolene. I met your father and brother last night." He wiped his forehead with his shirtsleeve. "I'm Dave. Me and my wife Alice own this place." Pride resonated in his voice.

"It's beautiful," murmured Jolene, looking to make a quick escape.

"We love it here," Dave replied, taking in the vast sky with a sweep of his eyes. "We'd always dreamed of owning this place, and two years ago our dream came true."

"That must have been wonderful."

"You can't even imagine." Dave continued on and Jolene slipped past the cottages, following the gurgling of water. Sadly, he was right. She couldn't imagine.

She ran from that thought, her feet pounding across the wooden bridge that traversed the Maitland River. On the other side, she veered left and raced down the trail until she reached a dead end at a small marina. Silver sailboat masts formed a web of lines and poles in the sky. The clang of metal came from within the maze of bright blue wheelhouses, and orange and white lifebuoys. Beyond the marina stretched Lake Huron, seemingly endless and blue. Jolene plunked down on the smooth wooden pier. Dipping the toe of her sandal into the lake, she watched the ripples radiate in a circle. Why did everyone else in her life know what they wanted except her? Why did she feel so lost and fragile?

Jolene hugged her knees to her chest. Hot tears rolled down her cheeks. One by one the tiny teardrops splashed into the deep blue waters of Lake Huron.

Chapter two

The soft padding of paws shook the pier. A coal black dog with tan markings on its muzzle and chest stood proud and alert behind Jolene. She had never seen a dog like it. Long ears dangled from its head and Jolene noticed that although it was muscular, angular ribs showed below its dense, short coat. "Hey boy," she called softly. The dog remained motionless. It wore no collar. She rose slowly to her feet. "Come here." The dog's muscles quivered as she approached. When she was close enough to discern the hopeful expression in its glistening eyes, it retreated, leaping from the pier with a graceful bound. "Are you hungry, boy?" she whispered. The dog's nostrils flared as if it could smell the mere mention of food before disappearing into the shadows of the neighbouring woods.

Alone on the pier, the mid-day heat enveloped Jolene and thirst thickened her throat. She retraced her path, her mind freeze-framing the expression in the dog's eyes. Back at the RV, she poured herself a lemonade and sat down at the computer, surfing the Internet for images of dogs. She stopped at a photo of a black and tan coonhound. "A working dog that runs its game entirely by scent," read Jolene aloud. "Courageous and proficient, outgoing and friendly. Some may be reserved but never shy or vicious."

Chaos rubbed against her feet and she fished an ice cube out of her glass, holding it in her palm while he played. When the ice had melted, she wiped her wet hand on his fuzzy back, sending him into a grooming frenzy. Jolene grabbed an apple from the crisper and paced. She hit the remote, heard the television buzz to life, then turned it off before a picture materialized on the screen. Her morning restlessness had returned. "There has to be something I really, really want to do," she told Chaos. A memory flashed in her mind — her mother perched on a stool, filling the cupboard above the refrigerator with art supplies. Jolene slid the stool across the floor, balancing on it while she rummaged for paint, a palette, a bundle of paintbrushes and a small canvas board. "Maybe I was meant to be an artist," she told Chaos, feeling a flutter of excitement inside her.

Lilacs and lavenders swirled in her palette. Jolene adjusted the intensity of the colour with dots of linen white. She dabbed the paint on the canvas, deliberating and experimenting with the length and pressure of her brush strokes. Patches of purple became flower petals. She lined the face of the petunia with smoky amethyst lines and dotted its stamen with thick golden dots of pollen. Chaos jumped onto the picnic table and sniffed. "Does it smell like a petunia?" she asked the kitten, tilting her head to regard her creation. Indistinguishable blobs of purple stared back at her. "Because it sure doesn't look like a petunia."

"What's a petunia?" asked Michael, coasting up behind her on his bicycle.

"This is supposed to be!" She gestured at the canvas with her paintbrush, splaying it with tiny droplets of yellow. "Oh great."

Michael took the board from her and flipped it upside down. "It looks like a spotted purple mongoose this way." Jolene snatched it out of his hands and her brother swallowed a smile. "You don't even like to paint," he reminded her. "You always complain when we have to do art projects."

The wind blew sighs through Jolene's hair. Michael was right. The art supplies were there for her mother, not for her.

"Guess what?" asked Michael.

"You found a swim team to train with."

His cheeks dimpled. "The Goderich Goldfins! The lady

at the pool called the coach for me. They practice tomorrow night and he said I was welcome to attend."

"That's great," said Jolene packing up squishy tubes of colour and trying to keep her voice even. She envied her brother's zeal for speed swimming. Their parents had registered both of them for swim classes when they were young. Jolene had liked the water and completed all her lesson levels, but Michael had been enraptured and had begged to join a swim team. Now he was a top-ranked age-group swimmer in Alberta. Jolene collected the palette and brushes. It wasn't fair. He'd lucked out. She cleaned the paintbrushes and left them on the table to dry, another thought preoccupying her. How had he known that swimming was for him? And how would she know when she found the right thing? "Michael, why do you swim?" she asked abruptly.

He shrugged his shoulders. "Why wouldn't I?"

His answer revealed everything she had already known. He swam because it was a part of who he was. He loved it — so much that he never questioned getting up for early morning workouts or pushing his body to exhaustion. "How did you know you wanted to swim competitively?"

"I don't know. It was just something I had to do." Disappointment flooded Jolene's features. It wasn't the insight she'd hoped for. "Don't you feel that way about your gymnastics?" Michael asked her.

Jolene fidgeted with the paints. "I've decided to quit." It was her first public admission.

"Really? I can't imagine giving up swimming. It's bad enough that my training's been disrupted by this trip."

Jolene hadn't expected him to understand. Nor had she expected the words that followed. "You're so talented, Jo. You'll be awesome at whatever you decide to do."

She smiled gratefully at him. "Thanks. I just wish I could find something that really appealed to me."

"Why don't you come try the swim club with me?" he suggested. "Speed swimming is totally different from lessons and you like the water."

"I'll think about it," she said, entering the RV. "Right now I have to finish my science project."

Michael winced. "Which I still have to start — later."

Chapter three

B y the time Grandpa returned, Jolene had finished her project on weather patterns in Canada and e-mailed it to the school. Michael was still trying to decide on a topic. "Why don't we take a walk and think about it," suggested Grandpa.

Sun-sparkled waves lapped at the wharf pilings and gusts of wind teased the water into small whitecaps. Jolene watched two enormous freighters docked on the opposite side of the harbour, their stacks dwarfed by five towering grain elevators. Small fishing boats bobbed along in the harbour amidst the noisy banter of fishermen. A flash of movement in the parking lot caught Jolene's attention. The coonhound she had seen earlier was slinking amongst the vehicles. "Hey! Get away from that fish!" A shrill whistle sounded and a rock hit the pavement. The dog ran off a safe distance and then returned, concealing itself beneath a nearby pick-up truck.

Jolene meandered in its direction, pausing while a tall fisherman lifted his small son to the wharf and handed him a cookie. He returned to his boat to unload his gear. The child spotted the dog and toddled towards it just ahead of Jolene. As the little boy bent down to peer under the chassis of the truck, his cookie fell to the pavement. The hound lunged for it and the child let out a piercing wail, sending the dog darting away and summoning the child's father. "That dog took my son's cookie!" He gathered the sobbing child into his arms. "Snatched it right out of his hand."

Onlookers encircled them. "Could have taken his little hand right off," stated one.

"I've seen that hound hanging around this past week," said another, "but it didn't seem aggressive."

"Must be hungry," said a woman's voice.

Jolene hung on the periphery of the circle. "Actually sir, your son dropped . . ."

Voices ricocheted around the wharf. "Can't trust a hungry dog . . . Got some food in the car . . . Looks pretty well kept . . . Providing it doesn't have rabies of course."

She tried again. "The boy dropped his cookie trying to . . ."

More high-pitched wailings filled the air.

"Any dog that would attack a youngster like that ought to be put down!" The voice belonged to one of the gruffest men Jolene had ever seen. Coarse silver stubble covered his cheeks and his face looked as if it had been chiselled from stone. He lumbered down the wharf like a bear coming out of hibernation. "There's no telling what it might do next time. That beast could have taken the child's hand or arm or worse." He paused for effect. "It could have gone for his throat."

Fear permeated the circle of onlookers. "You're right, Andy," said one voice. "It ain't safe to have a vicious stray on the loose."

"Our children are in danger."

Andy raised one gnarled hand, soliciting silence. "I'll call animal services tonight and tell 'em what needs to be done," he said, before limping away. People murmured in agreement. The discussion was closed.

Jolene gave Andy a wide berth as she made her way towards the end of the wharf. Michael was holding a life jacket and standing in a boat, obviously preparing to go fishing. She tugged on Grandpa's sleeve. "I'm going back to the RV."

"Okay," he said. "I'll hang around here until Michael gets back."

Jolene skirted the conversations on the wharf and headed towards the resort. She went first to the RV where she pilfered a leftover hamburger and some cheese, and then to the woods where she had first seen the hound. The creature's tracks were visible in the soft floor of the forest below the hill. "Hey pup," she called, knowing that its nose would detect the meal in her hand. For a moment, she envisioned the dog charging at her, ripping the food from her fingers, its fangs penetrating her flesh. She quickly rejected that thought. The child had dropped his cookie, the website had said coonhounds were never vicious and the dog's look of quiet hope had inspired trust.

Leaning against a moss-covered tree trunk, Jolene heard a squirrel's staccato warning pierce the silent shadows. Then she saw it, the soft tan patch on its underbelly illuminated by roving sunlight. The hound was standing only metres away, watching her. She slid her back down the tree trunk so that she was on the same level as the dog. Time slowed as she waited. The dog stood its ground. She stood hers. Finally, the salivating dog took two tentative steps in her direction. Jolene extended her hand so that the hamburger was fully visible. The dog shuffled forward until it was within an arm's reach. "It's okay, boy," she whispered. "I'm not going to hurt you." Letting the hamburger fall from her fingertips, she retracted her hand. The dog padded forward, snatched the food and devoured it. Its eyes never left Jolene's face.

Jolene held out the cheese, but dropped it when the dog refused to take it from her hand. It didn't trust her yet. This time, the dog carried it a safe distance before consuming it. When it was finished eating, it looked at her imploringly.

"I've got no more food, boy," she whispered. Returning to the RV, Jolene left the hound camouflaged in the woods.

Michael's voice summoned her to the door a short while later. "Hey Jo! Come see what I caught."

His grin was almost as wide as the brilliant silver fish in his hand. He lifted the fish's body and Jolene caught sight of a bulbous black eye. "Yuck!" she exclaimed. "What is that?"

"Supper!" proclaimed her brother proudly.

"Also known as a Coho salmon," added their grandfather.

"I caught it just outside the harbour. It put up a good fight," said Michael, reliving his catch. Brushing past his sister, he deposited the salmon in the sink, its fanned tail slopping onto the counter. Chaos let out a throaty purr and Michael picked him up. "I bet you'd like some of that, wouldn't you?" he asked, as the kitten's eyes became large emerald discs.

The strong smell of fish trapped inside the warm RV made Jolene gag. "Whew! It stinks." She inched the kitchen window open along its screechy runner.

"I'll cut some steaks," said Grandpa. He rifled through the utensils drawer, picked up the cutting board and knife, and retrieved the fish from the sink. Chaos stood meowing at his feet. "Come on, little feller," he told the cat, who pranced out the door after him. "You won't go anywhere so long as I'm slicing this up."

Jolene fanned the air in front of her with long slender fingers. "I wish you hadn't brought it inside." Standing on tiptoes, she tried to reach the skydome's crank handle. Michael came to her aid and fresh air wafted through the screen.

"At least Chaos is happy," declared Michael as they followed the cat and Grandpa outside. The kitten was trying to clamber onto the table in search of the deep red salmon flesh.

"He's crazy for it," said Jolene, as Michael lifted Chaos into his lap.

"He's certainly discovered something of interest," agreed Grandpa. Chaos gnawed at Michael's hand, but Michael held him firmly.

"How about you, Gramps?" asked Michael. "Did you find anything of interest this afternoon? You disappeared while I was fishing."

Before Grandpa could respond, Dad cruised up on his bicycle. "Look at that salmon!" he declared, eliciting the entire story for a second time.

Grandpa finished slicing the salmon steaks in time for supper. "You should see the Huron County Museum," Dad said as they crowded around the table. "There's an exhibit exclusively on the Great Storm. They've even got a pocket watch belonging to one of the captains and, believe it or not, his diary. It was on his body, inside a tight vest pocket, and it froze, preventing the water from soaking through. Rescuers found it when it washed ashore a year after his ship went down."

"Really?" asked Michael. "Could they read it?"

"Only the edges of the pages are water stained. All his notes are intact."

"That's amazing!" exclaimed Michael. "What . . ."

But Dad couldn't wait to share the rest of his news. "The curator of the museum is donating a box of clothes from that era for my exhibit and the Save Ontario Shipwrecks Society is trying to get me on a shipwreck dive."

"Awesome. Can I come?" asked Michael.

"You're not certified to dive," Dad reminded him. "Besides, I'll probably be gone a few days and there's always school to think about." He finished his salad. "Anything exciting happen around here?"

"Some dog attacked a little kid at the harbour," said Michael.

Jolene's fork clattered to the table. "No it didn't," she protested. "I was there; I saw it. The little boy dropped his cookie and the dog ate it."

Michael picked a bone out of his salmon. "That's not the story we heard."

"Apparently there's been a stray coonhound snooping around for the past week," said Grandpa. "It's tried to make off with the odd fish, but today there was the incident with the child." His gaze settled on Jolene. "The word is that it might be rabid. You'd be best to avoid it if you see it."

Jolene stared incredulously at her grandfather. He'd bought into the fear and hype just like all the others. And he hadn't believed one word she'd said. She opened her mouth to set the record straight, but the conversation had moved to Michael's swimming.

Chapter four

After supper, Jolene nudged the utensil drawer shut while Michael draped his wet dishtowel over the rack, his eyes on the television opposite the couch. "Ready to go?" asked Dad. He had promised to buy them all ice-cream cones if they helped him transport the clothing from the museum. He hated manoeuvring the RV through narrow streets. Dad tucked his wallet into his pocket. "Make sure you turn off the television, please," he said, stepping outside.

Jolene did so, leaving the remote on the table. Pulling her hoodie off her loft bed, she followed Grandpa and Michael outside. Summer's softness touched the night air. A buoy clanged in the distance, a rhythmic throb in the waning light.

Chaos stood on the step, purring pleadingly. "Sorry, but you've got to stay here," said Jolene, scratching him between his ears. She heard the kitten protest as she locked the door. "I hate it when he does that. He makes me feel so guilty."

"That's the whole point," said Grandpa.

They climbed the long hill towards the town centre, pausing occasionally while Dad photographed the harbour below them. On their left, the grain-storage terminals stood like cylindrical sentinels, supervising the unloading and loading of cargo. The small marina where Jolene had encountered the dog stood on the right-hand side of the harbour, and beyond lay the majestic waters of Lake Huron.

"What's that big dome-shaped building?" asked Michael, pointing at a steady column of vapour that marred the scene below them.

"The salt mine," Dad told him.

"Maybe that's why," said Michael, a dimple bordering his smile.

"Why what?" Jolene asked her brother.

"Why I keep expecting the lake water to be salty."

"Lakes are, by definition, fresh water," Dad reminded him.

But Jolene understood Michael's perspective. With nothing but water visible on the horizon, Lake Huron resembled an ocean. "It's so vast," she agreed.

The wind had died and they stood, watching the mirror-like surface. "And so peaceful," observed Michael.

"And so deceiving," remarked Grandpa, reminding them all of the reason for their visit in the first place — the storm that had claimed hundreds of sailors' lives in 1913.

"Superior, Michigan, Huron, Erie and Ontario," listed Michael, working his way from north to south on an imaginary map.

"And they're all connected," elaborated Dad, framing another photo. "Most of the ships on the lakes in 1913 were freighters powered by steam. The storm claimed many of them."

"Are there still ships wrecked on the lakes today?" asked Michael.

"Some, although today's vessels are much sturdier and equipped with GPSs and radios," explained Dad. "In 1913, only the newest ships had wireless radios aboard."

"So they had no contact with anybody while they sailed?" The idea seemed absurd to Jolene.

"That was a real problem," admitted Dad. "Two weather reports were sent out daily — one in the morning and one in the evening. The captains got them only when they were at dock. Once they were out on the water, all they could do was hope that Mother Nature would be merciful, and she wasn't always."

"No," agreed Grandpa. "Just ask those who knew the crew of the *Edmund Fitzgerald*. She disappeared suddenly in 1975."

"And there was the *Daniel J. Morrell*," said Dad. "She sank right here on Lake Huron in 1966. All crew members were killed except for one."

Jolene tried to imagine what it must be like to survive a shipwreck.

"Here we are," announced Dad, turning a corner. The Huron County Museum was a flat-faced, two-storey brick building with a large central door and latticed windows. They entered the lobby just before closing time and Dad set off to find the curator. Michael, Grandpa and Jolene waited beside a tall glass showcase displaying wildlife common to the area: white-tailed deer, hawks, squirrels and raccoons.

A few minutes later, Dad staggered towards them, balancing a large cardboard box full of clothing from the era of the Great Storm. The box was cumbersome, but by the time they'd reached the ice-cream shop, they'd figured out how to carry it without banging their shins. They left it outside and went in to survey the rows of colourful tubs. Jolene ordered first then slipped back outside with her cone to wait with the box.

Courthouse Square, an octagonal park with eight streets radiating out from it, was opposite her, and rings of light from the streetlamps illuminated the surrounding two-storey buildings. The Bedford Hotel with its corner tower covered one whole block and the courthouse with its classical ivory pillars dominated the park. Children's voices and the soft strum of a guitar drifted through the twilight.

Jolene leaned against the store window, trailing her tongue

across the soft purple ice cream. Her brother sauntered into the glow of the street light towards a poster-covered notice board. "Maple walnut?" Jolene asked, watching him pluck a nut from his milky white dome.

"Of course! Blueberry?"

"Naturally!"

She pressed her tongue into the creamy treat as Grandpa emerged from the shop, holding a cone topped with a strawberry pink swirl. Ice cream was an old and treasured tradition in their family. Dad would have chocolate and Mom would have something different every time. Jolene joined Michael, attracted by a poster of a girl twisting in a pike position. She turned away disappointed. The poster depicted a diver, not a gymnast.

Her brother tapped a notice advertising a missing girl. "Marissa Brighton," he read aloud. The girl had a whimsical smile and thick, auburn hair that hung in two braids to her shoulders. "Last seen July third right here in Goderich."

"Really? I didn't think kids disappeared in towns like this," said Jolene.

"Kids go missing all over Canada," Grandpa told them.

"Hey," said Michael, "she's just a few months older than we are."

The jingling of coins signalled Dad's arrival with his chocolate ice-cream cone. They ate, serenaded by the guitarist, then set off, carrying the long, flat box down the hill. "So have you given any thought to trying speed swimming?" Michael asked Jolene.

"You're taking up swimming?" queried Grandpa.

"I thought I might try it." Jolene glanced at Dad. "I don't want to continue with gymnastics."

Dad's eyebrows arched in surprise. "It's entirely up to you, Jolene," he told her. "I just think it's important to have something to call your own."

"I know," she agreed, impatience creeping into her voice. "I just don't know what that thing is."

Dad smiled. "It took me fifteen years of working as an engineer to figure out that I wanted to own a museum. I'd recommend you think about your strengths."

Jolene thought about that for a moment. She was a strong student but she was hardly passionate about fractions. She'd been a pretty good gymnast, but she hadn't liked it enough to continue. Michael always called her an ideas person, but ideas were so intangible. That, she decided, concluded her list.

"And I'd recommend you don't think about it at all," Grandpa advised Jolene. "It'll happen naturally, with experience, when the time is right."

While Dad and Michael rearranged the storage compartment of the RV, Jolene went with Grandpa to unlock the door. "When will the time be right?"

"That depends. People's passions and interests change as their lives change." He ruffled her hair. "You," he reassured her, "don't have anything to worry about."

Jolene wasn't so certain, but the noise in the RV pushed those thoughts from her mind. TV voices chattered in her ear. She flicked the light and punched the Off button on the remote, wondering how it had come to be turned on. "Chaos," she called. A plaintive meow came from beneath the front passenger seat.

Michael knelt down, peering into a tiny hollow. "He's here," he told his sister. Chaos meowed again as Michael pulled him out. His little body trembled and his eyes were wide and terrified.

"What's wrong with him?" Jolene stroked the cat's head and gradually he stopped quivering.

Dad stood in the doorway, looking quizzically at the twins. "Chaos was cowering under the front seat when we got home," Michael explained.

"And the TV was on," added Jolene, still perplexed.

Her father sighed. "I asked you to turn it off when we left. If you don't, the battery runs low."

"But I did!"

Dad stepped past them and tossed his wallet on the desk. "What happened here?"

Stacks of research files had been knocked from their tidy perch. Papers lay strewn about the floor. Jolene bent to collect them, speculating silently on whether or not Chaos was responsible for the mess.

"Those were all sorted and ordered," Dad groaned. He tapped Chaos' nose with his index finger. "You," he said, "have a perfect name!"

"How do you know it was Chaos?" asked Michael.

"He was the only one here," answered Dad matter-of-factly. "Besides, kittens are incredibly curious."

Jolene arranged the papers into a neat pile. "I don't know, Dad. You should have seen him. He was shaking with fear."

"Or guilt," said Dad, sitting down to reorganize his documents. "It's late. You two had better get ready for bed."

Life was full of mysteries, decided Jolene, as she climbed into her loft bed. Or at least today had been. Something strange had happened with Chaos. Before that there had been the dog, transformed into a vicious stray by false assumptions and fear. And there was still the question of finding something that she felt passionate about. Her eyes closed, her dream highway stretching long and formidable ahead of her.

Chapter five

The birds orchestrated the sunrise, awakening Jolene with an enchanting chorus of chirps. She dressed quietly and slipped outside into the pale light of dawn, hoping to find Grandpa whose bed was empty. Dewdrops glistened on coral rose petals as she made her way towards the office.

Dave, the resort manager, was sitting on the porch, sipping coffee and reading the newspaper. "Morning," he called to her.

"Good morning," replied Jolene. She was about to ask if he had seen Grandpa when she caught sight of the headline. *Vicious Stray Attacks Child.* "Is that article about what happened at the harbour yesterday?"

Dave closed the paper. "Apparently some hound dog tried to attack a little boy. Almost bit his hand off." Exasperation contorted Jolene's features. "Why?" asked Dave, reading her face.

"I was there," explained Jolene. "It didn't happen that way."

"Hmm," murmured Dave.

Jolene's neck and shoulders tightened. "What did they say?"

Dave cleared his throat and read from the article. "Following a vicious attack on an eighteen-month-old child, animal control officers are on the hunt for a stray coonhound last seen yesterday afternoon at the harbour."

"What will they do if they find the dog?"

"If it's aggressive, I imagine they'll put it down."

"But that's absurd. The dog isn't vicious."

Dave looked as if he were about to reply, but the telephone rang inside the office and he excused himself. Jolene didn't stick around. Anger simmered within her. It wasn't fair. The dog wasn't vicious or aggressive. It was hungry and probably lost. It needed a home, not to be put down.

In the harbour, a few small fishing boats puttered into the shade of the big freighters. The morning light spread like honey over the hills, and swallows perched like clothespins on electrical lines. Jolene mulled over what Dave had said. She had tried to tell the tall fisherman what she had witnessed, but perhaps she hadn't tried hard enough. She wandered along the dock, searching for the man and his young son, but found no familiar faces. Dejected, she headed home.

Grandpa was walking alongside the hedge that bordered the RV resort when she spotted him. She caught up with him as he ducked through a hole in the hedge that led to their site. Michael was dressed for a dip in the pool and Dad stood straddling his bicycle, ready to depart. He strapped his helmet on. "So what are you two up to?" he inquired of the twins.

"I've got that swim workout at five o'clock," replied Michael.

Dad turned towards Jolene, the same question in his eyes. She shrugged, her old anxiety returning to plague her.

"I'll be back by supper," Dad called as he pedalled away. "I'm sure you'll find something to do."

"You could paint another mongoose," suggested Michael. He ducked into the RV as Jolene winged her sandal at him. "Or me in the pool," he called back at her.

"Doesn't he ever get tired of swimming?" asked Jolene enviously. Grandpa collapsed into a lounge chair, holding a book on the history of Goderich, and Jolene retrieved her shoe. "I tried painting a flower yesterday," she told him, "but it was awful."

"Most first attempts are."

Jolene wrung her hands together. "But I don't have the patience to try another one. It won't work either."

"Probably not," agreed Grandpa, "although it might be

closer." He smoothed his moustache. "But I disagree with you. It's not patience you lack, just inclination. Why would you exercise patience to do something you don't want to do?"

Grandpa was right, but of no help. "So what do *you* think I'd like?"

"That's your decision, Jo."

"I don't want it to be my decision," she protested, causing Grandpa to smile broadly. "And I'm tired of thinking about it."

"So don't think about it then."

"But it's all I can think about."

Grandpa chuckled. "You need something to take your mind off your dilemma," he said carefully. "And I might know just the thing."

Jolene's eyes darted to her grandfather's. Something told her that he was harbouring a secret. Her heartbeat accelerated. Was Grandpa suggesting what she thought he was? "What's that?" she asked, her words steeped in hope.

"What's what?" asked Michael, jumping out of the RV and sensing his sister's anticipation.

"Gramps has found a time crease," said Jolene boldly. Although he hadn't admitted it, she suspected it was true.

"Really?" Michael leapt towards them.

Grandpa hesitated. "Yes," he admitted finally. "I've discovered a time crease." Excitement electrified the air. A time crease meant that they could time travel! These special creases were created by the energy of disasters — in this case, the Great Storm of 1913. Earlier in the summer, Jolene had accompanied her grandfather through a time crease into 1903, just days before a deadly rockslide in southern Alberta. And in August, she and Michael had visited Halifax in 1917 and been trapped by the chaos resulting from the explosion that had killed thousands. Grandpa had refused even to speak about time creases after that — until now.

Jolene studied her grandfather's weathered face. "Have you been back?"

He nodded. "Briefly."

"Can we go?" begged the twins together, knowing that Grandpa would be anxious to return to the history he loved and reluctant to leave them alone all day. "Please?"

Their grandfather deliberated. Jolene knew that if he said no, there was nothing the twins could do. Neither of them was able to see the hot shadows that marked the creases; only their grandfather could find them. "I suppose it would be good for your spirits," he said, eyeing Jolene who almost knocked his chair over in a hug.

Michael was leaping about like a gazelle. "We even have clothes," he cried, dragging out the box of clothing that they had transported from the museum last night. Reaching into the box, he pulled out a navy sailor's cap and pulled it down over his eyes.

Grandpa's moustache could not conceal his smile. "All right," he agreed. He scrutinized his grandchildren's faces, the mirth suddenly vanishing from his expression. "But this time, you will stick to the rules about using the time crease," he warned them. "I will not have you two getting hurt. Do you understand?"

"Okay," agreed Michael. "We'll go only with you. I promise."

"Me too," said Jolene.

"The Great Storm killed 244 sailors." Grandpa's eyes shimmered. "We'll be drawn back just days before November ninth, when the worst of the storm struck."

"Were any people on land hurt?" queried Jolene.

"The blizzard caused problems on shore, especially in the States," replied Grandpa, "but I don't think anybody was killed on land up here. Why?"

"Because then we'll be safe as long as we're not on the water, right?"

"That's right!" reaffirmed Michael.

The thought seemed to ease Grandpa's concern. "That's true. In which case, you are absolutely forbidden to set sail on any ships."

"Even if I have a sailor's hat?" asked Michael, lifting the brim of his cap and grinning.

"Especially if you have a sailor's hat!" Grandpa smiled affectionately at the twins. "All right. Let's see what kind of wardrobe we've acquired."

Michael rummaged in the box and handed him a charcoal wool suit jacket with three buttons, matching trousers and a vest. Jolene unpacked a white dress shirt with a high, rounded collar, a cardinal red tie and a creamy white Panama hat with a black silk band. "Classy!" she noted, passing them to Grandpa.

"Here," said Michael tossing Jolene a pale blue dress with a navy belt and cuffs. A pair of black leather lace-up boots landed at her feet, followed by a wide-brimmed white hat with a black velvet ribbon and rosette on one side.

"You've got to be kidding," she muttered, holding up the hat.

Michael clutched dark grey knee-length trousers and a grey sweater coat with cuffs and pockets. He sorted through the remaining clothes, selecting a cotton shirt and long navy socks to match his sailor's cap.

Jolene had already disappeared inside the RV to change. In the tiny bathroom, she adjusted the wide belt of her dress and did up the large pearl buttons that ran down the front of it between the navy piping. It reached almost to the top of her boots. She positioned the hat on her head in front of the mirror and laughed aloud. It fit perfectly, but it made her look as ludicrous as she felt.

"Sweet!" said Michael, taking in his sister's image as she emerged from the bathroom. He scratched at the woollen cuffs of his sweater coat and his short trousers. "These things are so itchy."

"Very stylish," insisted Grandpa as they joined him outside the RV.

They slipped through the hedge, crossed North Harbour

Road and followed a path half hidden by long, wild grasses. Grandpa led them behind the grain elevators and out onto a street, known as Harbour Road, on the south side of the harbour. The beach lay below them separated from the entrance to Goderich Harbour by a long concrete and steel pier. On the opposite side of the channel, Jolene could see the domed buildings of the salt mine. Where, she wondered, was the time crease?

Grandpa did not descend Harbour Road. Rather, he crossed it, leading them down a grassy knoll towards an abandoned red brick building with a large circular turret at one end and a triangular peak in the middle. Arched windows faced the harbour. "This used to be the Canadian Pacific Railway Station," Grandpa informed them. The station was situated at the base of a large hill adorned with a lighthouse.

"Is this where the time crease is?" asked Michael, stepping in and out of the shadows alongside the building.

"Yes," said Grandpa, his eyes suddenly alight. "Do you remember how a time crease works?"

"Time is a continuum, kind of like a long ribbon," recited Jolene. "One moment doesn't really end before another begins. Any specific instant on the continuum has the properties of the continuum itself."

"Which means," continued Michael, "that the past, present and future are not really separate times — they're all one."

"But energy . . . ," prompted Grandpa.

"Is not a continuum," declared Jolene. "And sometimes when there's lots of energy in a place, like when there's a disaster, that energy gets trapped in the time continuum."

"And forms a time crease," concluded Michael.

"Your great-great grandfather, who was a physicist in Italy, first discovered time creases," Grandpa reminded them. "To time travel, we fix ourselves in one location and let time pass over us instead of moving with time as we would normally do."

"Then the energy of the disaster pulls or pushes us through the crease," added Michael.

"Right." Grandpa smiled proudly at them. "Now stay close." He strode around to the rear of the station with the twins on his heels. They headed towards a dark shadow in a recessed doorway. Jolene felt the heat of the time crease as she stepped into the shade. She felt the shadows grow deeper, darker and thicker. Her skin grew tight and her body strained as if it were being stretched like an elastic band. She gasped as the air pressure increased, stealing her breath. Then, abruptly, she was yanked forward. A blast of heat sent her staggering into the light. Beside her, Michael swayed unsteadily, his chest heaving. Grandpa took a deep breath, dug a handkerchief out of his pocket and wiped his face. Ahead of them lay Goderich in 1913.

Chapter six

Horses neighed and Jolene jumped. A team of draft horses hitched to a wagon pawed at the earth, spooked by their sudden appearance. Voices chattered, and the twins and Grandpa ducked through an archway towards the station front. A covered wooden platform stretched the length of the building parallel to the railway tracks. Grandpa steered Jolene and Michael across them in the direction of the harbour. Only two large elevator terminals now blocked the sun, but a maze of wooden structures dotted the flat area at the base of the hill.

Jolene felt the ripples of exhilaration she always felt in the past — the excitement that came with experiencing something both new and old at the same time.

"It's so different and yet it's not," exclaimed Michael.

Grandpa led them across the flats, past the Ocean House Hotel, the lumber mill, the waterworks and power house and up onto the wooden wharf that ran along the edge of the flats. The wharf extended past the beach, and eventually turned into a pier, protruding out into Lake Huron. Smoke coiled upwards from the flourmill and the striped smoke-stacks of the ships docked in front of the elevators. A huge motorized leg dipped its buckets into the nearest ship's hold, extracted grain and moved it to a conveyor belt, which deposited the grain into one of the terminals. Jolene heard the delighted chirping of the little birds feasting on way-ward kernels.

She turned away from the noise and smoke and walked down the wharf in the direction of the lake. Women, wear-ing hats as ridiculous as hers, pushed prams over the worn boards. Men made their way in and out of the shops that lined the wharf — freight forwarders, fish shanties, and shops selling sailing accessories. An enormous freighter was enter-ing the harbour. Sailors, their caps pulled low over unshaven faces, stood at the railing. The incoming ship signalled its arrival with a steady whistle and Michael and Jolene turned to watch it glide past them. "They're massive," said Michael, taking in the full breadth and length of the boat.

Jolene stepped back as sailors and dockworkers filed past her. Her elbow bumped a girl about her own age and she muttered an apology. "No problem," said the stranger, flashing her a thin smile. The girl wore a cream-coloured blouse with a mint green skirt and a dark green apron overtop. The pocket of her apron bulged and bits of wax paper protruded from within it. On her head of thick, kinked hair was a wide-brimmed straw hat with two long tails of green ribbon fluttering from the back. As she approached the ship, she called to the sailors who greeted her with joyful exclamations.

"What's going on?" asked Michael.

Jolene shrugged. Boots tapped the planks behind them and they turned to see a young man struggling with a box and a curious contraption that resembled a wooden tripod. It was balanced against his shoulder and held in place by his chin. He clattered down the wharf with a noticeable limp, before setting his equipment down. Jolene could see that he walked on the outside of his left shoe, resulting in the uneven gait. Nearby, a rowboat had been secured by a coarse loop of rope over a wooden piling. The young man removed his woollen cap and wiped the perspiration from his forehead. Shrugging his jacket off, he laid it on the planks and placed his cap on top of it before lowering the box into the rocking rowboat.

Two boys, a few years younger than the twins, trudged down the wharf. "Hey George," called the blond one, a sneer on his dirty face.

"Learned to walk yet?" demanded his freckle-faced companion. George continued loading the boat.

"Don't you want to take a picture of us?" asked the blond boy, draping his arm around his buddy and posing.

George ignored them, ensuring instead that the box was well positioned in the rowboat.

"There must be a camera in there," whispered Michael to his sister. They edged closer so they could hear above the rumble on the wharf.

When George did not respond, the boys advanced. The freckle-faced boy leapt from the wharf onto a pile of near-by rocks on the beach while his friend kicked at George's jacket. George bent to collect his belongings but the blond boy was too fast. He plucked the cap off the jacket and stepped away, dangling it in front of George. "Nice hat," he quipped.

Jolene scowled and a frown creased Michael's forehead. George ran one hand through his sandy blond hair and lifted his jacket off the wharf. "Give me my cap!"

The boy swung it on one finger. "Come and get it," he taunted, holding it just out of the young man's reach. George lunged for it, but the boy backed away, deftly fling-ing the cap into a large puddle and sending his friend into a fit of laughter.

Jolene felt her anger swell like the tide. Beside her, she sensed Michael's fury and put a restraining hand on his arm.

Striding past the laughing boys, George clambered down from the wharf and stepped carefully onto a plank that bridged the puddle. Midway across, he bent to retrieve his hat and Jolene turned her attention back to the boys. The freckle-faced one scampered towards the rowboat, slipped the rope that secured it from its piling and threw it into the water.

"Hey!" cried George, almost losing his balance. "That's expensive equipment."

A loud splash reverberated from the harbour. Jolene watched as the blond boy dropped large rocks into the water, causing the rowboat to rock unsteadily, then drift out into the channel.

"Cut it out!" Jolene's shout came as rage urged Michael's feet forward. Another splash sounded, followed by the boys' mocking caterwauls. George started to manoeuvre his way back along the narrow plank, dragging his left foot awkwardly. Jolene and Michael broke into a run, leaping off the wharf onto the hard ground when they reached the puddle. The two boys raced down the beach, their taunts mingling with the screeching of the gulls.

The twins were now alongside the photographer and Jolene hesitated. George had almost reached the end of the board when he lost his balance, his arms circling wildly. Jolene leapt onto the plank, caught his arm and steadied him while Michael sprinted after the boys. George limped towards the rowboat while Jolene watched the chase along the beach. Suddenly the boys turned left into a maze of alleys that led through the flats back towards the ships.

Realizing that they would have to pass directly opposite her, Jolene started forward, hoping to cut them off. She caught sight of the two boys between two wooden shacks and picked up her speed.

"There they are!" screamed a girl's voice on her left. The aproned girl she had seen earlier was running parallel to her. The boys, having given Michael the slip, burst into a run and the girls followed them through narrow streets and past rambling buildings. But by the time they had reached the grain elevators, the boys had vanished.

Jolene hesitated. The low grumble of motors and the dusty smell of grain surrounded her. The girl with the apron slowed also. "It's no use," she said, peering into the shadows. "We'll never find them." She paused to catch her breath. "Simon and Harry are harbour rats. They know this dock better than the cats do."

Jolene brushed her damp hair out of her eyes and replaced her hat. She watched the panting girl beside her. She was taller than Jolene — wispy and thin in every way except for the reddish hair that ballooned around her face. She held her straw hat in one hand and pressed the top of the apron close against her stomach with the other. The girl raised one scant eyebrow and regarded Jolene with eyes the colour of the lake. "I'm Em," she said.

"Jo," replied Jolene. They smiled at one another. "I wish we'd caught them."

"Me too," said Em, pressing her hat back onto her mounds

of hair. "They're always bugging George, just because he has a club foot." They started in the direction of the wharf as Michael loped into view.

Jolene studied Em out of the corner of her eye. Her apron pocket was now less full and she jingled as she walked. "Is George your brother?" asked Jolene, matching Em's long strides. They had reached the place where Michael and George stood, assessing the situation of the drifting row-boat.

"Pretty much!" Em gestured towards Michael who had removed his jacket and laid it on the pier. "Is he yours?"

"My twin," replied Jolene.

"No way!" Em's eyes washed from blue to green to aqua-marine. Her gaze flitted from Michael to Jolene and back to Michael, the amused expression on her face changing abruptly to surprise. "What's he doing?"

Michael was in the process of shedding his shirt when the girls reached their brothers. He looked up at the sound of their footsteps, the button of his trousers undone.

"What's going on?" asked Jolene, alarm in her voice.

Michael removed his shirt, pried off his shoes and pulled off his socks. "I'm going in after the boat," he said without looking up. The lifeboat had drifted out into the lake, bob-bing in the water about ten metres off the pier. "I've got my swim trunks on," he reassured Jolene, blushing abruptly.

Jolene felt a wave of relief. Michael stepped out of his trousers, turned and dove gracefully off the pier into the waters of the channel. With long, powerful freestyle strokes, he swam towards the rowboat.

"He's a good swimmer!" exclaimed Em as Michael quickly reached the boat. Grabbing the rope, he looped it around his chest and began to swim breaststroke towards the beach.

"Wow!" said George. "Do you think he'd let me photograph him?"

"Do you think he'd teach me to swim?" asked Em.

"Probably," Jolene told them both as they hurried toward the beach to meet Michael. She watched her brother tow the boat, feeling a mixture of pride and envy. When the water was shallow enough, Michael stood and walked in, delivering the rope to George.

"Thank you," said George, inspecting his equipment, which was dry and unharmed. His almost-black eyes shone. "Do you want to come out in the rowboat with me?" he asked Michael. "I'd like to take some photos of you swimming."

Michael happily agreed.

"George is one of these new-age photographers," explained Em. "He believes in candid shots that catch the subject unaware."

"Exactly!" confirmed George. "By the way, this is Em, my sister. Em, this is Michael. He's new here."

"And Jo," said Michael, introducing his sister.

"Twins?" asked George.

Michael and Jolene nodded, wondering why anybody

bothered to ask. They looked so much alike — the same dark wavy hair, the same features, the same deep green eyes.

"And this is George," Em told Jolene. "And now that we all know each other, how about some toffee?" She pulled four wax-papered packets from her apron pouch and distributed them. George tore the wrapping from his and bit eagerly into the caramel-coloured candy. "Mary makes the best toffee this side of the Great Lakes," Em announced. "Every sailor in every ship that puts in at Goderich will tell you the same."

Michael sank his teeth into his toffee as Jolene twisted off a piece and popped it into her mouth. The sweet, rich flavour enlivened her taste buds. "Mmm," crooned Michael beside her, "this is delicious." Jolene nodded, savouring the scrumptious treat.

"Em sells it almost as well as mother makes it," remarked George. Jolene's eyes drifted to Em's apron pocket, remembering how it had once been bulging and how the sailors had crowded around her. Em stuck one hand into the pocket and produced a jangle of coins.

"Watch out for Simon and Harry on the way home," George told her. He dropped his jacket and cap into the rowboat. "Those two are trouble."

"Jo and I almost got them," said Em forcefully.

"And what would you have done if you'd caught them?" teased George.

Jolene wasn't sure. She had been so angry at their treatment of George that she hadn't stopped to think what she would have done with the two little bullies.

"I'd have sat on them and stuffed chewed-up toffee up their noses!" proclaimed Em. Laughter encircled the four of them.

"Well, I'm sorry you didn't catch them," said Michael, "but I'm glad you didn't waste this toffee."

Chapter seven

As their brothers rowed out into the lake, Jolene and Em strolled down the wharf amidst the stench of burning coal and the clanging of heavy machinery. "When did you arrive?" asked Em.

"This is our first day here."

"Want to see where I live?"

"Sure," said Jolene. "I'll just tell my grandfather."

They hustled along the weathered wharf. A woman pushing a pram paused to chat with Em, and Jolene slid past them to her grandfather, who was speaking to a sailor with a handlebar moustache. "Michael's gone out in a rowboat with George, and Em's going to show me where she lives."

"George? Em?" Grandpa asked.

"Mary and William's children," replied the long-moustached man. "Em's their new girl. She's a mysterious one, that one, but with a good heart." He winked at Jolene. "Mind, she'll say and do whatever she's thinking, though."

Jolene wasn't surprised. She rejoined Em who had managed to disentangle herself from the long lines of the woman's speech. "I hate babies," she muttered. "They burp and drool and gurgle and smell."

Jolene couldn't suppress a giggle. "They're supposed to be cute."

"How is being bald and smelly, cute?"

Jolene could think of no argument, so she changed the subject. "Do you sell toffee to all the ships that dock here?"

"And the trains," added Em proudly. "It was my idea, and soon I'll start selling at the sporting events."

Without warning, Em stopped and pressed her nose, lips and hands flat against the window of a shop. The man at the counter looked up and gave her a smile so broad that his eyes almost vanished. "That's William," said Em in response to Jolene's shocked look. "Mary's husband. He thinks I'm from another planet."

Jolene could see why and yet there was something intriguing about this unpredictable, uninhibited girl. She glanced up at the writing on the window that read *Ship Chandlery* and at the assortment of tools in the display case — charts, blocks and tackles, compasses, lights, whistles, anchors, coal scoops and more. William waved them off, and the two girls ambled away.

Jolene tried to piece together the information she knew about Em. "So William and Mary are your parents?"

"Sort of. I'm kind of an adopted daughter." Em leaned into the hill, climbing Harbour Road with strong steps. "My real mother died in Sarnia and I never knew my dad. I came to live with Mary and William a few months ago."

"Are they relatives?"

Em shook her head. "I'm still looking for my real relations."

They had reached the escarpment. A hawk soared above them and a spray of waves sent a silvery arch over the break-wall in the harbour below. Jolene felt the exhilarating thrill of heights envelop her. Her skin tingled and she felt a sudden urge to leap off the cliff and soar.

"John's out there somewhere," said Em.

"Who's John?"

"Mary's oldest son. Celeste says he's got water in his veins instead of blood. All he's ever wanted to do is sail."

"Who's Celeste?"

"Oh, you'll meet her."

On the hilltop, a park adorned with fall colours awaited them. Off to one side sat a wooden bench beneath a brilliant canopy of crimson and pumpkin-coloured maple and oak leaves. The wind gusted, whipping the girls' hair into their faces as they continued past an inn and picnic area.

"Have you seen Courthouse Square yet?" Em asked. "Or the Bedford Hotel?"

Jolene pictured the square as she had seen it yesterday night. "Not really," she answered, wondering if it would be greatly changed.

"We'll go by our house first," said Em, leading the way. "Then I'll give you a tour."

Em turned right on Wellington Street and stopped at an elaborate Victorian style house of brick. Three storeys rose up from the ground to a large tower crowned with cast iron cresting. The roof, with four sloping sides became steeper as it descended over the ornate window mouldings. Jolene stared at it in awe. Em continued past the front doors around to the side of the house while Jolene waited in the street, admiring the details of the home and wondering how old it might be. A plaque near an upper-floor window engraved with the date 1879 answered her question.

Emerging with her apron bulging, Em led the way towards the square. It was different, but not as changed as Jolene had expected. Eight streets still branched out from the park and a courthouse stood at its centre. Except this was an older version of the courthouse — a large, imposing building adorned with pillars and a cupola and clock. Directly across from it, Jolene recognized the Bedford Hotel. Covered buggies pulled by horses were parked next to an antique-looking car. The bell tower clanged twelve times and Em pulled off her hat and broke into a run. "Let's go see Celeste. She'll be on her lunch break now."

A young woman wearing a fur-trimmed coat and a full-length dusty rose dress was leaving the hotel as they approached. She paused to pull on soft black gloves and adjust her velvet hat. Black lace shaded her face and black feather plumes rose from the hat's brim. She was a picture of elegance and style.

"Celeste," called Em, dashing in front of a horse and buggy. Jolene sprinted to keep up with her as the driver reined his horse in.

"Hello Em," said the young woman. Her lips curved upwards in a burgundy smile among fine-boned features.

"Are you going to the post office again?"

Pink bloomed in Celeste's cheeks. "You sound like George," she said trying to sound cross, but her dark eyes twinkled. Loose blond curls framed her pretty face and faint freckles dotted her nose.

"I knew it," Em said. "By the way, this is Jo."

Celeste nodded at Jolene and gracefully descended the steps, her pointed black shoes protruding beneath her hemline. "It's nice to meet you," said Celeste. "And I'm glad to see you're sensibly wearing your hat." She looked sideways at Em.

"I've got too much hair for this silly thing." Em swung her hat in her hand.

"You wouldn't if you'd let Mother cut it or me teach you to style it." The heels of Celeste's shoes clicked as she stepped into the shade. "And if you don't protect your skin from the sun, you'll end up with freckles."

Em turned her face rebelliously towards the sun. "So!"

Celeste sighed. "Never mind. Oh, tell Mother that Mrs. Harper wants more toffee," she added before crossing the street.

"She's very pretty," observed Jolene.

"I should hope so!" exclaimed Em. "She spends every spare penny on those silly concoctions, trying to be more prettiful." She scrunched up her nose. "That ought to be a word," she told the two chestnut horses that stood attached to a nearby buggy.

"Really?" said Jolene. "When she's already so beautiful."

Em rubbed the velvety muzzle of one of the horses. "Freckles aren't in fashion," she said with a dramatic sigh. "As if women don't have more important things to think about! She's been like this ever since she got engaged." Em gazed into the chocolate brown eyes of the animal. "George says it's love that's made her stupid." The horse neighed in understanding.

"Have you met her fiancé?" asked Jolene as they resumed walking.

"No, but as soon as the sailing season's done, Edward — that's his name — has promised to come."

Jolene glanced up at the trees. Most of the leaves had turned and many already lay scattered about the park. "Will that be soon?"

"Most of the captains try to be off Lake Huron by mid-November. They don't want to get caught in a winter storm.

They'll be on their last trips of the season 'round about now."

"Celeste must be so excited."

"Oh yeah," Em assured her, rolling her eyes. "Unbearably so." They laughed together. "I wish she'd go back to university and finish her medical degree as she intended to before she met Edward."

"She left school to get married?"

"Lots of girls do. It's as if they don't believe that they should have the same opportunities and rights as men."

"But she went into medicine and there aren't many women doctors," observed Jolene. "Besides, she can always go back later."

"Except she won't!" Jolene wondered how Em could sound so decisive when the decision wasn't hers. "Uh, oh," Em muttered, a dark look crossing her face.

Harry and Simon were prowling across Courthouse Square. They flattened themselves against the courthouse wall, looking as if they were about to stage an ambush.

A young girl, her chestnut hair falling like string down her back, came into view, just ahead of the boys. In her hands, she held an open book.

As soon as she had passed them, Harry and Simon fell into step behind her, just out of her sight. "Look! It's Frannie Bananie," Simon hollered, cupping his hands around his mouth and bellowing. Frannie made no response.

Em ground her teeth together. "Frannie's deaf and mute,"

she explained. She indicated a path around the courthouse that would allow them to reach the boys unseen and the girls sprinted off, the boys' mocking words in their ears.

Harry jostled Frannie, swiping the book from her hands as the young girl gestured frantically at him. "Little Women," he pronounced, reading the title aloud. Em and Jolene crouched low, scurrying among the trees in the park until they were adjacent to Simon.

Simon put one hand on his waist and wiggled his hips in an exaggerated feminine walk. "I'm a little woman," he called, fluttering his eyelashes. "I can mend your socks."

Harry held the novel out of Frannie's reach and fluffed up his greasy hair. "I'm a little woman," he sang out in a soprano voice. "I can iron your shirts."

Frannie jumped for the book, which Harry promptly launched over her head to Simon. The girl mouthed a soundless protest. She stamped her foot indignantly.

"That's how all women should be," decreed Simon. "Silent." He resumed his female masquerade. "I'm a little woman. I can bake you a pie," he said, tossing the book back to Harry.

Fuming, Jolene and Em leapt from their hiding place. Jolene intercepted the book mid-air and Em grabbed Simon's shirt collar. "I'm a little woman," she declared. "I can kick your butt!"

Harry was already retreating, casting wary glances at Jolene. Simon wrenched away, his collar ripping completely off his shirt. He dashed after Harry. "Coward!" screamed Em. Dropping the scrap of material, she ground it into the dirt with the heel of her boot.

Jolene returned the book to Frannie, who signed appreciatively to both of them and re-opened her novel.

"The worst part," said Em, as they resumed walking, "is that those two rats learned their attitudes somewhere. Which is exactly why women need to speak out and celebrate their achievements. Look at Mary Pickford, the talented actress, or Pauline Johnson, the native author." She skipped ahead of Jolene. "And what about Nellie McClung, the great spokesperson for women's rights?"

As they turned right on East Street, Jolene marvelled at Em's ardour. She had obviously discovered what she really cared about. For the second time that day, envy prickled Jolene. "Where are we going?" she asked trying to ignore the emotion.

"To meet the train."

"I thought the station was on the harbour flats."

"This is the Grand Trunk Railway and hopefully there will be some hungry passengers on board when the train arrives at 12:40 and other hungry people waiting to depart."

It was a good system and Jolene found herself admiring Em's business strategy. Her new friend mingled easily with the passengers waiting for the incoming train. A coil of smoke and a low chugging signalled the steam engine's arrival. A conductor stepped off the train and helped the passengers disembark. Em hustled among them. She stopped to speak to two young women carrying placards that bore the slogan *Give Women the Vote*. Jolene realized that they must be suffragettes.

When Em rejoined her, her pouch was empty except for coins. "I wish I could go to a suffragette rally!" she said, her eyes ablaze. "But Mary thinks I'm too young."

They passed the Bedford Hotel, where Jolene could see Celeste at the reception desk, and other two-storey commercial buildings: the Huron House Hotel, the telegraph office, theatres, the newspaper office, a photography studio, the bank, drug stores, a barbershop and even a confectionary advertising ice cream. The side streets were lined with elaborate stone buildings — churches, the town library and the stately Victoria Opera House. Beyond the square, were residential homes, many of them just as elegant and luxurious.

"I'd better go and find my grandfather and brother," said Jolene.

"Okay! Maybe I'll see you tomorrow at the Thursday market?"

"Uh, sure," agreed Jolene.

Em's stomach emitted a low growl, sending her feet marching in the direction of her house before Jolene could find out any more details.

Chapter eight

Letting the incline of the hill determine her momentum, Jolene soon found herself bounding past the flourmill onto the wharf. She resisted the urge to turn cartwheels on the smooth boards, contemplating her decision to give up gymnastics. She missed the physical activity and the training routine, but she didn't really miss the sport itself. It was time for something new.

She spotted Grandpa outside the chandlery shop, speaking with a man wearing wire-rimmed spectacles, and headed their way. Michael arrived from the opposite direction at the same time. "Hello," called Grandpa. He turned to the man beside him. "Mr. Clarkson, these are my grandchildren, Jolene and Michael. This is Mr. Clarkson, the harbour master." Wrinkles folded into the man's face like an un-ironed shirt.

"Twins!" exclaimed Mr. Clarkson, eliciting a polite nod from both Jolene and Michael.

"And what have you been up to?" Grandpa asked the twins.

"George took me down to the boneyard," said Michael, unleashing Jolene's imagination and causing her to grimace.

"Ah, the old ship graveyard." Mr. Clarkson grinned. "And did you discover any stories?"

"Not as many as Gramps would have," admitted Michael.

A rueful smile crossed the old man's face. "Those were the unlucky ships."

"Have there been many?" asked Jolene.

"The first big vessel ever to set sail on the Great Lakes was the *Griffon,* named after a mythical creature with an eagle's head and wings and the body of a lion. I always imagine it as a sort of dragon. The *Griffon* had a cargo of furs and a crew of seven and she was supposed to travel up Lake Huron to Green Bay. But a violent storm took her to the bottom on her maiden voyage. And there she lies to this day — the dragon of the lakes." Mr. Clarkson paused. "I sailed the Great Lakes for thirty years and never without thinking about that dragon. When the creature sleeps, it's as gentle and meek as can be, but when it's riled, it can lash out at you with an intensity that can overpower even the most skillful captain and crew."

Tiny waves dotted the lake. Jolene imagined them to be vibrations from the dragon's snores.

"Couldn't ships shelter from storms here?" asked Michael.

"Goderich is the only deep water port on the east side of Lake Huron. We'd like it to be a harbour of refuge, but I'm afraid that's not the case at the present time."

"How come?" Michael was curious.

Mr. Clarkson pointed to the breakwater that protruded into the lake and marked the access to the channel. "In my opinion, the entrance to the harbour is too shallow."

"But how would you fix that?" asked Michael.

"If it were up to me, I'd dredge the harbour basin and make it deeper. Then I'd move that breakwater away from the shore and extend it farther into the lake. Big vessels need deep water to steady themselves."

"Wouldn't that be expensive?"

"How much is a life worth?" Calloused fingers pulled a handkerchief from a pocket. Mr. Clarkson removed his glasses and blew on the lenses. "And that foghorn we have on top of the waterworks building ought to go, too."

"You don't want a foghorn?"

Mr. Clarkson polished his lenses. "On the American side, the foghorns are compressed air horns operated by small, gasoline engines. You can hear them a lot farther off shore than the one at Goderich. It's no more than a whistle really. And it ought to be out on the breakwater. No point trying to steer your ship through the flats is there, son?"

"Doesn't the lighthouse help?" Michael gestured to the lighthouse perched on top of the hill.

"Yes, but it's a steady light."

"You'd see it more easily if it flashed or blinked."

Mr. Clarkson clasped Michael's shoulder. "If only you were the one I had to convince," he said with a despairing laugh.

Grandpa looked at the sun sliding slowly down the sky. "It was a pleasure, Mac, but we ought to be going." Dad would be back by suppertime. They said their goodbyes and made their way towards the time crease.

"What did you do today, Jo?" asked Michael.

"Explored," replied Jolene, "and I met Em's sister and saw two suffragettes."

"You mean women still can't vote?" Shock raised the pitch of Michael's voice.

"Women in Ontario didn't win that right until 1917," Grandpa told them "and only after a lot of persistence and inspiration from suffragettes like Nellie McClung."

Em had alluded to Nellie McClung earlier that day and Jolene had read about her charisma and persistence. Jolene wondered if she would have had the strength and determination to be a suffragette. She wondered if she would ever have the passion and drive to be as influential as Nellie McClung or as passionate as Michael or Em.

Grandpa looked thoughtfully out at Lake Huron, which, in the sun, resembled a thousand liquid diamonds.

"When will the storm hit, Gramps?" asked Michael, drawing Jolene's attention away from her own preoccupation.

"The worst will be in four days' time."

Jolene shuddered. The dragon was sleeping now, but she knew that it would awaken in the rains and storms. Her dad's next exhibit was testimony to that.

They reached the railway station and ducked beneath the archway. The horses that had witnessed their appearance were destined to witness their disappearance. Jolene followed her brother and grandfather into the time crease with mixed emotions. Without the energy of the storm, they could not time travel and yet that same storm would cause terrible destruction. She gripped Grandpa's arm and the pressure of the time crease sent her thoughts fleeing. Once again, she was caught in the passage from the past to the present.

Inside the RV, Michael pried off his boots, and stripped off his 1913 attire, revealing his long swim trunks. "I can't believe you wore those," said Jolene.

"It's a good thing I did," replied Michael, referring to the rowboat rescue. He downed a glass of juice while Jolene set her hat on the table and unlaced her boots. Ducking into the bathroom, she changed into her swimsuit.

Grandpa propped the door of the recreational vehicle open. The odour of fish still lingered. "I'll put the clothes away," he offered. "You go ahead and have a swim."

"Thanks Gramps," called the twins. They raced to the pool, kicked off their sandals and dropped their towels on the lounge chairs.

Jolene hesitated at the sight of a sign that read *No Swimming when Lifeguard not on Duty*, but Michael seemed unfazed. "Dave hires a lifeguard during the summer," he told her. "Dad and I spoke to him yesterday and he agreed that we could use the pool once Dad had vouched for our swimming ability." Michael pulled his shirt over his head while Jolene regarded the tiny pool. She couldn't see the bottom of it. "The previous resort owner was also a deep sea diving instructor," explained Michael. "When he had the pool built, he made it deep enough to train underwater divers."

Michael dove and Jolene jumped in, feeling her body descend. She swam, twisted and somersaulted through the water, letting its cool clarity refresh her. Finally, she followed Michael's ring of bubbles to the surface. "Guess what?" he said. "I've decided on a topic for my science project."

"What?"

"I'm going to do a report on the Great Storm and all the shipwrecks." Michael cupped his hands together and squirted water in Jolene's direction.

"You could tie it into weather forecasting or navigation in the past, and Dad could help you with the research."

"Good ide . . ." Michael sank beneath the water, his last syllable a gurgle.

A shadow fell across the pool and Jolene swam to the

edge to greet Chaos and her grandfather while her brother swam backstroke with long, easy strokes.

"What a scorcher!" Grandpa said, fanning himself with a book as Jolene hoisted herself out of the pool and stretched out on her towel. Grandpa set Chaos on the concrete and the kitten headed for the pool's edge. Catching sight of his reflection in the water, he tilted his head first one way and then the other, before lowering a curious paw into the water. Ripples distorted the image and Chaos retracted his paw, his bright eyes attempting to follow every wave.

Grandpa's chair scraped loudly across the concrete and Chaos jumped. He landed on the lip of the pool and teetered there for a moment, before losing his balance and slipping into the water. Flattened ears, astonished eyes and a flurry of white feet emerged seconds later.

Jolene leapt to her feet and dove into the water, her body arcing gracefully, her hands penetrating the water in a natural streamline. In three strokes, she had reached Chaos and lifted him to the pool's edge.

Michael joined them. "Cats," he declared, laughing, "are not water-resistant."

"You poor little thing," Jolene said, consoling the sopping wet cat. She scrambled out of the water and wrapped Chaos in Michael's towel so that only the kitten's eyes and nose were showing.

"He'll be fine," Grandpa assured her. "And I must say that dive had fine form."

Reluctantly, Chaos succumbed to Jolene's gentle towel-ling. Then, shaking and fluffing, he turned his back on them and began to groom himself.

Michael climbed out of the pool and picked up his towel, now covered with ginger-coloured hair. He dropped it in a heap at his feet. "So what's Em like?"

"Intense and different," said Jolene thoughtfully.

"How so?" asked Michael, reclining in the sun to dry.

"I don't know. There's just something unusual about her." Jolene struggled inwardly to understand her comment. Em was definitely intense, but she was also unusual. It was as if she were too . . . she searched in vain for the right word.

Chapter nine

The sun beat down on the pavement, heat rising in undulating waves. "It's too hot to sit out," announced Michael, jumping back into the pool.

Jolene agreed. "Come on," she told the kitten, getting up and heading towards the RV. "I need a drink."

A truck with an Animal Control Services logo on the driver's door rolled towards her and a man dressed in a khaki green shirt stuck his head out the open window. "You haven't seen a coonhound moseying around here have you?"

This was the officer who was hunting the dog, with the intention of putting it down. "A coonhound?" stammered Jolene.

"Yeah, a black and tan dog about thirty centimetres high at the shoulder. It was last seen yesterday afternoon at the harbour."

Jolene stared at the reflection of herself in the man's sunglasses. "No sir," she replied, dropping her eyes. The lie seared her stomach.

"I've left a live-bait trap on the other side of the bridge that crosses the Maitland River," he said, eyeing Chaos. "You'd be best to keep your cat away from that area until we trap the dog. I expect we'll have it by tomorrow morning." The truck accelerated slowly past Jolene. Guilt needled her skin, but her conscience retaliated. How could she just hand over an innocent creature to someone who might kill it when it wasn't even a threat?

"What did the guy in the truck want?" asked Michael, catching up with her.

"He was looking for the dog that people say attacked that kid at the harbour." She turned desperate eyes on her brother. "The hound isn't vicious, Michael. It didn't happen the way everyone thinks it did."

"I don't see that there's much you can do about it," said Michael, racing ahead.

While Michael showered, Jolene pulled a sarong over her swimsuit and considered her brother's comment. The stove clock registered 2:54 p.m. as she grabbed some pepperoni sticks and an apple and hurried in the direction of the Maitland River bridge. She had to find the dog before it found the trap.

A simple single-door steel contraption had been set up on the fringe of the woods. Jolene noted with relief that it was designed to trap but not hurt the animal. A hunk of raw meat had been placed inside. Jolene had a vivid vision of the hound enclosed in the cage, its eyes beseeching her to release it before it was killed. She glanced over her shoulder. There was nobody in sight. She listened for footsteps or voices but heard only the gentle rush of wind in the trees. Cautiously, she approached the steel cage, loathing the injustice of its presence. Anger bubbled inside her. The dog didn't deserve this. Savagely, she kicked the trap twice and then jumped aside as the lid slammed shut. Her feet carried her into the woods, away from the steel trap and towards the innocent creature she felt the need to protect.

Positioning herself against the mossy tree trunk, Jolene settled down to wait. If the animal control officer had been searching for the dog today, it might be wary. But she sensed its presence within moments. "Come on, boy," she urged, waving the pepperoni stick. The dog came within an arm's reach but did not take the food from her hand. "Okay," she conceded, dropping the meat, "have it your way." She placed the apple on the forest floor and watched as the hound came to retrieve it. "This isn't the best diet for a dog," she apologized as it licked its lips, "but it's a lot safer than that hunk of meat in the cage."

As Jolene passed the trap on the way home, trepidation rose within her. Setting off a trap was probably a criminal offence. But she'd been right to protect the dog. It was innocent and safe — at least for the moment — and now she had some time to think of a more permanent solution. She thought about confiding in Grandpa, but rejected the idea. He'd specifically told her to avoid the dog if she saw it.

Grandpa was reading copies of old newspapers when she returned and Michael was hard at work on the computer. Dad had left things out to make lasagna and Jolene began preparations in the hope that the task might distract her. She tossed the ground beef in a skillet and mashed the small clumps of meat with a wooden spoon. On her way to the fridge, she paused behind her brother's shoulder. "What is that thing?" she asked, pointing at the monitor. It showed a picture of a flag with a black square in the centre.

"A storm signal," replied Michael.

"Really?"

"That's what it says."

"Predicting the weather has sure changed with technology," observed Grandpa. "The new maps and charts give accurate movements of even gale-force winds."

"Those maps are so confusing," said Michael, bringing up a weather map on the screen. "Something about highs and lows and which way the winds blow."

"High pressure areas circulate clockwise and low pressure areas counter-clockwise over Canada." Jolene had included that in her weather project. "And the prevailing winds here blow from west to east." She stirred the hamburger. "Storms are typically generated when . . ."

"Ants carry eggs to high ground and cats sneeze," finished Michael, stopping Jolene mid-sentence.

"What?"

"That's what it said on one site about how animals predict the weather."

"There's likely some truth in those old indicators," said Grandpa.

Jolene was skeptical. She added a jar of pasta sauce to the skillet and mixed cottage cheese, an egg and parmesan together in a bowl. The area around the Great Lakes was prone to storms, which weren't always easy to forecast. Storms, she knew, form when two air masses collide. Low-pressure air masses are generally associated with rainy, changeable weather and high-pressure air masses with fine, settled weather. If a warm mass of air runs into a cold one, the warm air rises, cools and the moisture in the air condenses into clouds and rain. Jolene layered the lasagna noodles, meat sauce, and cheese mixture. She hadn't done any research on the Great Storm of 1913 though, and she was suddenly curious as to why that storm had been so much worse than others. She'd have to ask Michael when he was done.

After grating the mozzarella cheese on to the lasagna, Jolene slid the pan into the refrigerator. It was still too early to cook it. Picking up Chaos from his patch of sunshine, she made her way to a Caribbean-coloured hammock strung between two chestnut trees and fell into it. The kitten

curled up against her shins, placed one paw over his eyes
and purred contentedly. Jolene looked up at the hill on the
other side of the river, wondering where the coonhound
was now.

"Hey sleepyheads!" Dad grabbed the hammock, swinging it
wildly and waking both Jolene and Chaos.

Grandpa was setting the table, and Michael was in the
process of shutting down the computer. "Did you have a
good day, Doug?" asked Grandpa.

"Excellent, but tell me about yours first." Dad dropped
his wallet, keys and camera on the desk.

"Ours was great!" said Michael. Jolene glared a warning
from behind an oven mitt, but her fears were unfounded.
"We did some exploring around the harbour, watched some
freighters being unloaded and met a few locals." Mischief
twinkled in Michael's eyes. "I met some sailors and a photographer, and Jo met this girl named Em."

Jolene slid the pan into the oven, her feelings an incon-
gruous mixture of amusement and guilt. It wasn't fair that
Dad couldn't time travel. According to Grandpa and her
great-great grandfather's journal, not everyone could use
time creases. Grandpa thought it had something to do with
being able to see and feel the energy of history, something
Dad couldn't seem to do, even though he was the one with
the museum. So far, neither she nor Michael nor Grandpa
had shared their secret with anyone.

Michael tapped Jolene on the shoulder. "We'd better go if we're going to be on time for swim practice." Jolene hesitated. Part of her wanted to go, but part of her suspected it would all be in vain.

"Go ahead," said Dad.

Trying to hide her reluctance, Jolene packed a swim bag. Michael was waiting impatiently outside at their bikes. "Have fun," called Dad as they rode out of the campsite. Grandpa waved, but said nothing.

All was quiet at the RV when Jolene coasted into the campsite twenty minutes later. She could hear the drone of the television inside. "Speed swimming not your thing?" Grandpa asked from the shadows.

"No," Jolene admitted. "I didn't even try." She dropped her bicycle on the grass and flopped down beside it. "I just don't have it, Gramps. I don't have the drive it takes to swim like Michael does."

"Why would you," asked Grandpa letting the book fall against his chest, "devote your strength and energy to an activity you don't care about?" Jolene plucked blades of grass from the lawn as Grandpa resumed reading about the ships that had sailed across the Great Lakes into history.

"The lasagna's ready," Dad called as Michael arrived home and they took their places at the table.

"Delicious," Michael told his sister. Dad and Grandpa nodded in agreement.

"I'm going to do the Great Storm of 1913 for my science project," Michael told Dad halfway through supper.

"What a coincidence! The Great Storm Exhibit is still at the Huron County Museum, but I believe it's supposed to start travelling again soon. Why don't we bike up and see it?"

Riding through the streets of Goderich after supper, Jolene contemplated taking up cycling as a sport. She liked her bike, but she wasn't crazy about riding on the highways as she'd seen other cyclists do in training. Besides, autumn wasn't a good time to take up a summer sport. A late breeze, like an afterthought, stirred the leaves as they parked their bicycles outside the museum and went inside.

While Michael made notes on the Great Storm Exhibit and Dad poked about the archives, Jolene and Grandpa wandered through the hall that resembled a historical town. A polished train engine was on display, surrounded by storefronts. In the photographer's studio, they could see a bellows-style camera mounted on a wooden tripod like the one George had used. Jolene and Grandpa wandered past an old fire hall, jeweller and watchmaker's, printer, dress shop and the undertaker's office. How many caskets had they needed in November of 1913, wondered Jolene.

When Grandpa stopped to talk to a volunteer, Jolene passed through a room of ship models and found herself in the Great Storm Exhibit.

"Hey Jo," Michael said without turning as she came up behind him.

"How'd you know it was me?"

"By your step, your rhythm, the way you breathe."

Jolene looked fondly at her brother. That was one of those things they could never explain to people who weren't twins. "What did you find out?"

"That the Great Storm was really two storms that collided and formed a hurricane." Michael pointed at the map. "On November seventh, an intense low system caused a storm, mainly over Lake Superior." Michael's fingers indicated the largest and most northern of the Great Lakes. "Then two days later, a system blew in off the prairies, bringing extremely cold Arctic air with it. When the cold air collided with the deep low, the temperature plunged. The moisture turned to snow and winds picked up causing a hurricane and blizzard on November ninth."

Jolene frowned. "There are lots of storms on the Great Lakes. What made this one so great?"

"Wind speeds exceeded 120 km/hr, waves rose to eleven metres and there was a whiteout snow squall, all of which lasted for approximately sixteen hours," offered Michael.

"And the air masses absorbed a lot of moisture from the lakes, which were unusually warm that fall." Dad had come up behind them. "When that turned to precipitation, it caused horrendous ice to form on the ships."

Jolene recalled the sunny warmth of her afternoon with Em. It was hard to imagine that in just a few days' time in 1913, those same ships in the harbour might be covered in ice.

"Enough homework for tonight?" Dad asked Michael.

"Totally," agreed Michael. "Let's go home."

Home was a disaster when they arrived just after sunset. The fridge door had been unlatched and the milk, eggs, salad and leftover salmon strewn about the vehicle.

"But Chaos can't even reach the handle," protested Michael in the kitten's defence. "And he looks scared again."

"He's got a reason to be scared after making this mess," growled Dad. He indicated a tea towel hanging on the door of the fridge. "All he had to do was pull on this and the door would have opened." Dad used a paper towel to sop up a broken egg.

When the mess had been cleaned up, Grandpa turned on the television to a program about the Missing Children's Society of Canada. A picture of a girl in braids flashed onto the screen and Jolene thought she recognized her.

"Isn't that the girl we saw on the poster uptown?" asked Michael.

"Marissa Brighton was last seen in the town of Goderich, Ontario, approximately two months ago," said the host of the show. "She was a foster child who had lived in a number of different homes since being placed in the care of social services almost ten years ago." The image of the girl in braids faded into a picture of a bewildered toddler. "Anyone knowing the whereabouts of this thirteen-year-old girl, who is believed to have run away, is asked to contact their local police department."

Jolene changed into her pajamas, lifted Chaos up onto

her loft bed and climbed up after him. Mysterious problems were everywhere. The mystery of Marissa — the missing girl — had never been solved. Jolene hoped that she could solve hers. All she had to do was find a way to save the dog, get Chaos off the hook, and discover her passion in life. It was enough to make anyone tired. She closed her eyes, hoping that she would not dream about the highway again.

Chapter ten

The ring of a cell phone and Dad's quick response woke Jolene. "Where are you going?" she whispered.

"A fellow from the Marine Historical Society is picking me up. We're going to drive down the coast to get some photos of lighthouses and the sites where the wreckage was found after the storm."

"Were there ships wrecked all over the lake?" asked Jolene, sitting up in bed and avoiding the ceiling. Chaos squirmed sideways into her warm spot.

"Pretty much," whispered Dad. "Most of the bodies washed ashore on the Canadian side south of here because of the winds." He strapped his watch onto his wrist. "Eventually I'd like to do a 3-D model of the lake showing the location of all the shipwrecks, kind of like the computer one Michael's doing for his project."

"Huh?" asked Michael in a sleepy voice, having heard his name.

Dad left after instructing them to eat the leftover lasagna for supper and to be sure to do some schoolwork.

"Schoolwork," groaned Michael, propping himself up on one elbow. His hair was a heap of out-of-control waves. "I bet Mr. Clarkson could answer all my questions about weather and sailing in 1913."

"Sounds good to me," said Jolene encouragingly.

It didn't take much to persuade Grandpa. By eight o'clock they were dressed and ready to go. Chaos sat on the windowsill looking longingly outside. "Can we bring him, Gramps?" asked Jolene, stroking the kitten's head. "He's dying to be outside."

"How will you keep track of him?"

Jolene thought for a moment. She slipped her hat off and dropped Chaos inside. He sniffed, then curled up. "See, he likes it." Her eyes pleaded with Grandpa.

"Besides," added Michael, "if we leave him and he makes another mess, Dad will go ballistic."

"That's true," agreed Grandpa. Jolene still wasn't convinced that Chaos had been the culprit, but having persuaded Grandpa to let her take him, she said nothing. Tucking her hat and its passenger into the crook of her arm, she followed Grandpa and Michael out the door and down to the railway station.

The same team of horses whinnied as the threesome materialized from nowhere into 1913. The horses' wagon was full of boxes of apples and sacks of potatoes. A whistling young man came out of the station, looking mildly surprised to see them. He stepped up into the driver's seat.

"Good day," said Grandpa.

"Morning," came the response in a rich tone that resounded in Jolene's ears.

"Those are fine looking apples." Grandpa admired the shiny red fruits.

The boy, probably a few years older than Jolene and Michael, ran a tanned hand through his jet-black hair. The muscles in his bare arms rippled as he gathered the horse's reins. Jolene thought him extraordinarily handsome. "For the market," he replied.

"Em told me about it," interjected Jolene. "We should go."

"It's in Courthouse Square," said the driver. "I'd be happy to give you a lift up."

Michael leapt into the wagon and Jolene followed, positioning herself beside a box of polished apples. Chaos poked his head out of her hat and sniffed at the cargo. The young man offered Grandpa a hand up into the driver's box and then looked back over his shoulder. He flashed a brilliant, white smile at Jolene and she felt her head spin. "Now there's a sweet thing," he said, still looking back into the wagon with brown eyes so dark that they seemed to be all pupil. Colour flushed Jolene's neck. "Just young but you couldn't walk by and not notice that one." Her cheeks burned and she fidgeted with the buttons on her dress.

"His name's Chaos," said Michael's voice. Jolene's gaze dropped to the kitten in her lap. She looked away trying to hide her embarrassment and felt the wagon lurch. What a fool she was. As soon as the wagon stopped, she scrambled down, leaving Grandpa and Michael to thank the driver.

Courthouse Square had been transformed into a mass of activity. Small, makeshift booths lined the sidewalks, and wagons and carts dotted the road. Boxes of carrots, potatoes, squash and apples stood in stacks as women, children and men scurried back and forth, carrying their wares.

"Jo!" Em's voice called out in the midst of the hubbub. "Over here." Jolene caught sight of a willowy arm waving and she and Michael hastened in that direction. A round, ruddy-cheeked woman wearing a sapphire blue dress and a matching hat was setting jars of jams and jellies out in a wheelbarrow. Em stood beside her, holding a box brimming with toffee.

"Hi Em," said Michael. "What are you selling?"

"Duck!" shouted Em.

"Duck?" queried Michael.

Em grabbed his sweater coat and pulled him towards her. "Duck." A man with an enormous sack of beets swung around narrowly missing Michael's head. Jolene giggled and soon they were all laughing.

The woman put a protective hand on her table of jams as the beet man struggled to pass by a cart of sheep. "Why Em," she said, registering the twins' presence, "these must be the new friends you and George were telling me about yesterday." She straightened up, although at full height, she was still shorter than Jolene, and extended a hand to each of them.

"This is Mary," said Em, "and these are Jo and Michael, the twins."

Mary clasped their hands in her dimpled ones. "Welcome," she said with a smile that seemed ten sizes too big for her. Jolene liked the small space between her front teeth and the way her deep-set eyes resembled two bright stars. "Em tells me you're new to Goderich."

"We came with our grandfather," offered Jolene.

"I believe William met him yesterday at the harbour. Said he was a real gentleman. Off you go and fetch him now," she directed Michael. "Tell him to come and say hello."

Just then, Chaos let out a loud meow, demanding attention for the first time since their arrival. "You've got a kitten," said Em. She reached into Jolene's hat and picked him up, her eyes wide and dreamy.

Mary scratched the cat's ears with a chubby finger. "He's adorable," she said. A voice hollered and Jolene heard a heavy thud behind them, which startled Chaos. "Here," said Mary, handing Jolene an apron embroidered with tiny roses. "I'll bet he'll fit into one of those pockets."

Jolene tied the apron behind her back and Em slid the kitten into the middle pouch. Immediately Chaos poked his head up, curled two white paws over the edge and purred happily.

Michael reappeared with Grandpa, and Mary greeted him, warmth radiating from her smile, her touch, her words. She insisted that he and the twins join them for supper that evening and Grandpa agreed on the condition that the three of them assist her at the market. Mary, her eyes twinkling in a jolly round face, was quick to accept. She pivoted in a tight circle and handed the box of toffee to Jolene. "Jo can start selling toffee and you others can help me set up." Jolene placed her hat on an empty crate and stuffed the toffee into the pockets on either side of Chaos. The kitten pawed at them, intrigued by the rustling of the wax paper. Beside her, Em and Michael were busy creating a table from some old crates.

Mary pointed towards a young woman pulling a toddler by the hand. "Here's your first customer," she told Jolene. "They're two for a penny."

By the time the child had eaten his toffee and petted Chaos, the kitten was a sticky mess and Mary and Grandpa had set out most of the preserves. Chaos retreated into the apron pocket to groom himself. More customers arrived and Jolene was kept busy with toffee sales. She put the pennies into Chaos' pocket and could hear him batting them around. Em and Michael had begun unloading baked goods: cinnamon buns, lemon and apple pies, blueberry tarts and rich teacakes.

"I love blueberries," said Em, setting a tray of tarts on the table.

"And strawberries," said Jolene.

"How about you, Michael?" asked Em.

Michael thought for a moment. "Berries are good," he announced finally, "but my favourite fruit is pomegranate."

"Yuck! I can't stand all those little seeds," Em sang out.

Mary bustled towards them, holding a ten-dollar bill in her hand and sending Michael off to the bank for change.

Em pulled a small, black drawstring pouch from her apron, withdrew a black-and-white photo and propped it against a blueberry pie. "Who's that?" asked Jolene, staring at the man in the photo. Thick dark hair had been combed back from the man's broad-beamed face. Piercing eyes stared back at Jolene from amidst classic features, and a large distinctive birthmark coloured one cheek.

Em avoided her question. "This photo was with my mother's things." Mary's busy hands stopped for a moment. She watched out of the corner of her eye as Em flipped the photo over and showed Jolene the inscription on the back. *Love Frank.* At the bottom of the photo, *Goderich, Ontario, 1910* had been written. "There's no last name, but the photo was taken here three years ago, so I keep hoping somebody will know him."

"Who's Frank?"

Em shrugged. "A relative, I'm guessing."

There was no time for more questions. Customers had started to arrive in droves. Michael returned from the bank with coins jangling in his pockets. While Mary called out prices and greetings, the three children selected and packaged goods, making change when necessary. Jolene caught snatches of dialogue in the bustling market ". . . those new talking pictures were absolutely wonderful . . . need a curfew, we do . . . Should have seen the comedians in the opera house . . . Mr. Russell's been ill, a bad of case of shingles . . . last run up the lake and then they'll be home." Grandpa stood beside the booth, chatting amidst the clucking of chickens, and the aromas of fresh-baked bread and smoked sausages.

Finally, the market-goers began to subside. Mary, her cheeks much redder than they had been earlier, removed her hat and fanned her face. Her hair, Jolene noticed, was braided, wound into a bun and pinned up. It was the rich colour of pecans with only a few wisps of grey above her ears. "When she lets it loose, it reaches to her knees," whispered Em into Jolene's ear. "But I've only seen it like that once."

"Em," called Mary, "why don't you open that last cinnamon twist. I think we all deserve a little something." She turned her palms to the sky. "I swear that I make enough every time, but I never seem to."

"Perhaps if they weren't so scrumptious," said Grandpa, tasting the piece of cinnamon twist that Em had just passed him.

"Mary's stuff is the best in town," bragged Em.

"Hush now," said Mary. "You're just a biased child that's all." But her eyes shone. "Besides, I still have a jar of jelly and two fruit cakes left."

"Sounds like a midnight snack to me," said a voice behind them. Jolene recognized it as belonging to the harbour master they had met yesterday.

While Mary wrapped up the cakes and jelly, Grandpa greeted Mr. Clarkson. "We were hoping to find you today," he told the harbour master. "Michael wanted to know about the navigational devices sailors use and I thought you might be able to help him."

"I'd be glad to," replied Mr. Clarkson.

Michael bounded to his side, but Grandpa looked back at the market stall. "Maybe we could help Mary with these crates first."

"Don't you worry about that," she declared. "The girls and I can finish up." Em stuck her tongue out at Michael.

All around them, people were repacking unsold goods, loading carts and stacking crates. Em slipped the photo of Frank back into her bulging drawstring pouch, making Jolene wonder what else it contained. She pulled the squirming kitten from her apron and dropped him onto the grass where Chaos immediately became intrigued by a row of ants carrying crumbs. His paw descended. He raised it then replaced it over the frantic insects. Jolene turned back to the clean up. Ants could keep a kitten busy for hours.

Chapter eleven

After gathering up Chaos and the crates, the girls followed Mary down West Street. Em hummed a song that seemed vaguely familiar to Jolene, but whose title escaped her, and Jolene pushed the loaded wheelbarrow. Despite her plumpness, Mary's pace was brisk and the girls soon found themselves languishing behind. Jolene admired the homes around them, in particular a large, stately corner house. "Hey," she said, squinting into the sun, "isn't that Harry and Simon?" The two boys were bent over, scurrying alongside the picket fence on the side of the house.

"Come on!" cried Em, setting her crates on the corner of an intersection. Jolene parked the wheelbarrow beside them and sprinted to catch up with her. "What are they doing?" she whispered as the boys opened the gate.

"Borrowing Mrs. Ostrom's dog," Em replied through clenched teeth. Strutting up the walkway behind the boys, she asked loudly, "Well, well, what have we here?"

Harry had slipped a rope around the old bulldog's collar; however, the dog seemed oblivious to the boys' presence. It continued to doze in a sunny patch on the porch. Simon whirled around, his eyes darting to an open window on the first floor. "Uh, we were just returning Butch here," he lied.

"I see," said Em. "So I expect you'll now be notifying Mrs. Ostrom that her precious dog is back home." Butch opened one eye and regarded her sleepily.

Harry shrugged, his feet already in motion. "No need," he said giving the girls an artificial smile, "consider it our good deed for the day." The two boys took off, leaving the rope dangling on the stairs.

Em bent down and pulled it free of Butch's collar. "There you go, Butch," she said. The dog's head remained firmly supported by the warm deck boards.

"What was that all about?" asked Jolene as they closed the gate behind them.

"Mrs. Ostrom is this wealthy widow who probably has Alzheimer's disease. She's completely devoted to that silly bulldog, so the boys have devised this scheme. First they let the dog out of the yard and then they return it for a reward. Mrs. Ostrom doesn't remember that the same thing happened last month."

Jolene had to admit that it was ingenious — devious but ingenious. "They must have to carry Butch away," she said, grinning at the thought of the bulldog's inactivity.

They were almost at the corner of the intersection when the storm in Em's blue eyes began. Her crates had been upset and the wheelbarrow re-parked in the middle of the intersection. Jolene raced to grab it as a motorcar approached. She reached for a sliding wooden box, the corner of another one hammering her in the elbow. The driver tooted the horn as Jolene, her load jostling, hustled towards Em. "That was close," she said, surrendering to a giggle.

But Em was not amused. "If I ever get my hands on those two rats," she said, ferociously twisting her hair into a ponytail.

Jolene watched the storm rage in Em's eyes. "There's no damage to the crates," she offered, feeling that her friend's reaction was a little extreme.

"It's not about the crates!" Em's feet pounded down the sidewalk. "Simon and Harry constantly terrorize and exploit the old, the weak, the disadvantaged." Jolene thought of George's clubfoot, Frannie who was deaf and mute, and the elderly widow. "Those are the people who need to be hassled the least in life. Trust me, I know." She kicked at a rock. "And worse, those boys will grow up to be demeaning and abusive to women because they think we're inferior."

Jolene listened thoughtfully to Em's tirade. She couldn't see the connection between the mischievous boys and abusive men, but she kept her thoughts to herself. They sauntered past the post office. A horizontal stone banding decorated its exterior and stone lintels lay across the tops of the door and windows. A steady stream of people came and went. "Celeste," Em called as her sister, wearing a daffodil coloured dress with a wide, black belt descended the steps.

"Em! I got a postcard from Edward." Celeste waved a postcard depicting a lighthouse at the girls. Her dark eyes beamed and her hair glistened. She pressed the postcard to her heart and seemed to float away.

Em watched her go. "I wish she'd just forget about him," she said disdainfully. "It's terrible what happens to females when they fall for some guy."

Jolene was less inclined to be so hard on Celeste. Her thoughts drifted to the handsome boy driving the wagon.

When they had finished stacking the crates in the backyard, Jolene followed Em into the kitchen where Mary was sliding a roasting pan into the oven. Chaos was restless, clawing at Jolene's pouch. "What should I do with him?" she whispered to Em.

"Close the doors and let him explore," suggested Mary, overhearing her. "I'm sure he'll find something to amuse himself with or a cozy spot to sleep."

"You don't mind a cat in the house?"

"We've had cats every since I can remember. John took our old tomcat, Toby, on the *Wexford* last time he set off. They were having mice problems."

Jolene followed Chaos as he explored the kitchen with its

large coal-burning range, square icebox, copper-bottomed kettles and steamers, milk strainers and butter churns. He upset a whiskbroom and scampered into the parlour as it clattered to the floor. A matching sofa, armchair and two reception chairs, their polished mahogany arms and legs gleaming, encircled a large throw rug. Jolene watched Chaos investigate the legs of the piano, sniff at the large stone fireplace and then duck into an adjacent room where a dining table was covered with an intricately embroidered tablecloth.

"Want some soup?" asked Em from the kitchen. She dipped a ladle into a pot simmering on the stove. "It's a Mary's special, which means it could be anything." Em set bread and butter on the table and the two girls ate hungrily.

"Oh good. I see you've had lunch," said Mary, passing through the kitchen into a small pantry. Jolene and Em could hear her rummaging for something.

"What are you looking for?" asked Em.

"Mrs. Harper's basket of toffee. I thought I'd have you and Jolene deliver it."

"Uh, we could do that tomorrow." Both Mary and Jolene watched Em closely. "Right after I make another batch," she added weakly. "I took it to the market."

Mary's tongue tsked. "Maybe Jolene would help you."

"Sure," said Jolene. Em looked relieved.

She lifted a cast iron pot onto the stove and dug something out of the icebox before disappearing into the pantry.

"We need butter, vanilla and brown sugar," she said, holding up each ingredient as she named it. "And two secret ingredients — Lily white corn syrup and Eagle Brand condensed milk."

"That's it?" How could something so delicious be so easy? Jolene made a mental note to remember the ingredients so she could make it at home.

While Jo melted the butter and stirred in the sugar, Em added the final two ingredients. She took the spoon from Jolene. "And now we stir for just the right amount of time."

While Em stirred the toffee, Jolene rolled her dress sleeve up to examine the deep purple bruise on her elbow where the crates had bumped her during her wheelbarrow rescue. "I'd sure like to teach those two hooligans a lesson," said Em. Her lake-blue eyes narrowed. "Maybe we could trap them."

"With toffee?" joked Jolene.

Em's eyes bulged. "Yes!" she exclaimed. "That's a great idea." Jolene could feel her scheming. "But not just any toffee — special toffee."

"Special toffee?"

Em handed Jolene the spoon and disappeared into the pantry. She re-emerged with two bags and held up one — a sack of black pepper.

"Won't they notice?" asked Jolene, imagining the dark pepper flakes in the creamy brown swirl.

"Not if we add walnuts," said Em, displaying the other

bag. "Mary makes it that way sometimes." She set a smaller cast iron pot on the stove and Jolene scooped a small portion of the mixture into it. Em added walnuts first and then two heaping spoonfuls of pepper. Watching Em's gleaming eyes, Jolene decided that she never wanted her as an enemy.

By the time the girls had finished the toffee and cleaned up, they had two separate batches — one for Mrs. Harper and a special one for Harry and Simon. They cracked the toffee once it had set, and wrapped the pieces in wax paper, placing the peppery ones behind the basket in the pantry. "I can hardly wait!" said Em.

Chapter twelve

Once the kitchen had been tidied, Mary asked Jolene and Em if they would fetch William, Michael and Grandpa for supper. The girls found them in William's shop. "Did you get your homework done?" Jolene whispered to her brother.

"Uh, huh. Mr. Clarkson knows all about sailing and weather."

Jolene studied the harbour master's wrinkled face. Did he know that very soon the worst storm in the history of the Great Lakes was going to hit Lake Huron? She glanced at Em and William and Mr. Clarkson. What would happen to them? None of them was a sailor. None of them would be on the water. But William's oldest son, John, would be.

William closed up shop and Mr. Clarkson led the way up the hill. He paused at the top. "I guess I'll be getting on home," he said, but Jolene could hear the reticence in his voice.

"Nonsense," exclaimed William, slapping the older man's shoulder and guiding him towards his house. "We're already privileged to have guests and there's always room at the table for another." Mary, catching sight of them through the window, had already placed an extra plate on the table by the time they entered the house. Celeste and George were home from work and the house was warm and noisy.

Jolene and Em helped serve dinner, positioning the dishes around the table. After setting a bowl of beef broth out for Chaos, Mary joined them. Dinner was as delicious as Jolene had expected it to be. Juicy roast beef, rich smooth gravy, buttery carrots and puffy golden Yorkshire puddings. Two apple pies were served up for dessert along with well-steeped tea. Nursing her tea, which was too strong to drink, but lovely to hold, Jolene listened to the lyrical tones of the conversation in the parlour.

"It looked like you had a good day at the market," commented Mr. Clarkson.

"It's Em," said Mary, a hint of embarrassment in her voice. "She's got all these money-making schemes and they always work." She laughed. "Not that we aren't fortunate enough, but I suppose every bit helps."

"A little extra never hurts. Celeste still has another year of university," said Mr. Clarkson, looking at Celeste, who was perched on the piano bench. Beside her sat a Victrola with its large trumpet-like cone projecting into the room. A wide black disk that Jolene recognized as an old record sat on the turntable.

"Actually, Mr. Clarkson, I've decided not to return to university this year."

"Really? I heard you had excellent grades. You'd make a splendid doctor."

Celeste shifted awkwardly. "Edward and I are planning to get married in the new year."

"Well, well, let me be the first to congratulate you then."

"Thank you," said Celeste, blushing attractively.

"It's a stupid idea." Em's voice was full of contempt. "If Edward really loved you, he'd let you finish school first and then get married. If you ask me, he's an insecure and selfish man."

Celeste bit her bottom lip, her beautiful facial features displaying her hurt and confusion.

"Nobody asked you, Em," Mary said firmly. "I suspect that when you are old enough to understand the nature of love, you will think otherwise."

Em scoffed but stayed silent.

"Besides," said George. "Celeste can always go back to school after she's married." He caught his sister's eye. "I'm still waiting for you to find a cure for my clubfoot."

"And I will," declared Celeste, looking reproachfully at

Em. "It's not as if I've abandoned my dreams; I've just re-ordered them."

Grandpa set his teacup down. "As I was telling Jo the other day," he said, "you'll pursue your passion when the time is right."

Jolene nodded her honest agreement and Em threw her a look that labelled her a traitor.

Grandpa deftly changed the topic. "Your father tells me you're hoping to have your own photography business one day, George"

"If I can afford it. Photography equipment is expensive and I'll need to buy a car as well. But I figure that if I need money, I can always ask Em," he said.

Everyone chuckled, except for Em. "There should be a good toffee market at the hockey games this year," she said seriously.

"I hear the Sarnia team is strong," added William. "They start their season next week."

Jolene could almost see the dollar signs in Em's eyes. "Aren't you going to Sarnia this week, William?" asked Em. "I could go with you."

"I am planning a trip," he admitted.

Mary sighed. "My sister's there with three young children and a husband who's away on the lakes. I suppose you could lend her a hand," she said. She frowned abruptly. "But I don't like the idea of you at the rink, Em. It's no place for a young girl alone."

Mr. Clarkson interrupted before Em could articulate her

rebuttal. He gestured at a studio portrait of a young man who bore a striking resemblance to William. Jolene reckoned it must be John, the eldest child, and Mr. Clarkson quickly confirmed her thoughts. "Any word from John?"

"Not since we saw him when the *Wexford* was last in for repairs." Mary's eyes fretted. "I've heard rumours that she was leaking, Mac. Do you think that's the case?"

"Well, I'm no inspector, Mary, but I think the *Wexford's* as good a vessel as sails these lakes. I spoke to Captain Patterson when he left and he figured they'd be back on the weekend. I suspect that'll be his last run of the season and John will be here to trouble you for the winter again very soon."

"Won't that be lovely," said Mary. "All four of my children home." Jolene noted that she included Em in that count.

William obviously noticed the same. "It seems like just yesterday that you arrived in that silly blanket," he said, addressing Em.

"You were a mystery," admitted George.

"So are you planning to stay then?" inquired Mr. Clarkson of Em.

"Yes sir, at least until I locate my relative."

"Ah yes. The young man in your picture." Mr. Clarkson set his saucer on his lap. "I meant to tell you that a sailor I spoke to yesterday knew of a Frank who matched his description. The word is that he's just signed on with the *Regina*."

"The *Regina*? Do you know her?"

"I certainly do. She's a package freighter captained by Edward McCallum, a good friend of mine. She'll be heading up from Sarnia in the next few days."

"Will she stop here?" Em balanced on the edge of her chair.

"Not likely," said Mr. Clarkson. "Generally the freighters sail up the American side."

"But she'll be in Sarnia this weekend?"

"I believe so."

Em turned towards Mary. "Please Mary, can't I go with William? Then I can see if the *Regina's* in dock and meet Frank. Please." She pressed her hands together in a praying gesture.

Mary's fingers drummed lightly on her teacup. "I don't like the idea of you going off to meet strangers, even if they are family."

William chuckled. "She met us and we were strangers."

"Not stranger than Em," teased George.

Laughter warmed the room but Jolene noticed that Celeste did not join in.

Mr. Clarkson rose. "That was a lovely meal, and I particularly enjoyed the company." His gesture included the entire room. "But I best be getting back to my old dog. He'll be wondering where his dinner is." An image of the coonhound flashed through Jolene's mind and she stood up.

"We, too, should be going," said Grandpa, rising. "Thank you so much for everything."

Mary beamed with pleasure. Jolene carried her teacup into the kitchen and looked about for Chaos. He was not in the kitchen or the parlour. While Michael searched the pantry, Jolene followed Em upstairs to her bedroom. The curtains and bedspread were a spearmint green and a beautifully embroidered angel, done in delicate pastel colours, hung on the wall. The whole room looked as if it had been touched by spring.

Chaos lay curled up on Em's apron, which she'd hastily thrown on the end of the bed. He rose and stretched, first his back paws and then his front ones. Em scooped him up, his claws catching in her apron. It fell and Em's black drawstring pouch skimmed across the polished floor. Jolene watched as it came open and a small, silver object slid towards her feet. She stooped to pick it up. "Why do you have a cell phone?" she asked Em in amazement.

Em grabbed it from her hand, her eyes just as shocked. "How do you know what it is?" she demanded.

"Oh good! You've found him." Michael burst through the door, plucking the kitten from Em's hands. "Hurry up. Gramps is waiting." He tugged Jolene's arm, pulling her down the stairs and out the door, her mind numb with wonder and confusion.

Chapter thirteen

Twilight was descending on the backs of the clouds as Grandpa and the twins returned to the RV resort. Jolene clutched Chaos in one hand and the apron that Mary had given her in the other. Her mind was a blur. She could only vaguely recall saying her goodbyes or passing through the time crease.

Michael immediately commenced work on his computer model of the shipwrecks during the Great Storm. "I'm going to start with Lake Superior and work my way south," he told them. Jolene dug out her math, but found herself unable to concentrate. The triangles, hexagons and circles on the page kept transforming themselves into an image of a cell phone.

"You seem distracted," said Grandpa when she joined him outside. "Are you still doubting your ability to be passionate and driven?"

Jolene shrugged. "Em's certainly passionate about the things she believes in."

"A little over-zealous, wouldn't you say? She really offended Celeste tonight."

"At least she knows she has the fortitude to stand up for what she believes."

"And so do you," Grandpa reassured her. Jolene wasn't so sure, but her mind was too overloaded to dwell on it.

Dad barged through the door about a half an hour later. "Good news!" he cried. "I'm going on a diving expedition to see some of the shipwrecks from the Great Storm. We leave from Sarnia early Sunday morning and return to Goderich Tuesday night. Can you imagine the great underwater shots I'll have?" His voice withdrew into the refrigerator. "Didn't you guys eat?" he asked. "The lasagna's still here."

"We ate out tonight — at a friend's place," Grandpa said carefully.

Dad looked surprised. "Anybody I know?"

"Remember that girl Jo met yesterday — Em?" said Michael, coming to the rescue. "Her mom invited us all for dinner."

"Well, that was nice," said Dad. "Perhaps your new friend would like to pay us a visit, Jolene. Not that I'm a great chef or anything, but maybe a sleepover in an RV would be appealing."

"Uh, thanks Dad," said Jolene. "I'll keep that in mind." Out of the corner of her eye, she caught Michael's amused look.

"I'll have some lasagna, and unless you're all too full, we can go for ice cream," offered Dad. Jolene saw Grandpa's shoulders relax and felt hers do the same. It was awful having to deceive her father.

She stroked Chaos' back. He was lying on her binder, but it didn't matter. She couldn't focus anyway. Instead she found herself thinking back to her time in 1913 — to the market, making toffee, supper at Em's. Everything had been perfect until . . . Jolene flipped the cover of her math book open and closed. How had Em acquired a cell phone? Had it come through a time crease? Perhaps from a recent shipwreck? Jolene was still perplexed when they left, leaving Chaos sleeping on her books.

Michael began to recap what he'd learned that day. "Two boats disappeared on Lake Superior," Michael told them. "In one case, the captain was in such a hurry to leave that he set sail without waiting for the cargo hatches to be properly closed. The waves swamped the boat and filled her hatches."

"A case of bad judgment," reflected Dad.

They walked in silence and although Jolene tried to keep her thoughts on other things, they returned again and again to Em and her mysterious cell phone. It must have passed through a time crease. Em must have discovered it and kept it as a curiosity. Jolene's eyebrows knit together. Yet her friend had been shocked when Jolene had identified it. That must mean Em also knew what it was, but that would have been impossible in 1913.

They reached the ice-cream shop, where the line-up stretched right out the door. "Why don't I order," suggested Dad, "and you can wait out here. The usual?"

They all nodded. Grandpa accompanied Dad into the shop while Michael stooped to pat a yellow Labrador tied to a lamppost. Jolene leaned against the corner of the notice board. For the hundredth time that day, she pressed rewind on her mental videotape, searching for the details that didn't quite fit. There was, of course, the cell phone, but there were other things that had made Em seem unusual. Something about her mannerisms, her language, her attitude. Jolene replayed her mental tape again. Some small detail was bothering her. "Michael, did Em say she disliked pomegranates?"

"Yeah, I think so," he replied as the dog licked his face.

A strange brightness stole into Jolene's eyes. Pomegranates. How would Em have ever eaten pomegranates? They were an exotic fruit and she'd only lived in Ontario. Even if they did ship pomegranates to North America in 1913, which she highly doubted, they'd never have arrived in an edible condition. And Em had mentioned Alzheimer's, which probably hadn't even been identified in 1913. And that song she'd been humming — it was an old Beatles' remake, and they weren't that old. She whirled about, looking for Michael who was no longer petting the dog. He was studying the missing persons photo on the notice board. Jolene's eyes followed his gaze. She gasped. The name was different, but names were easy to change and if the hair hadn't been braided . . . Marissa Brighton could just be Em.

"Michael," whispered Jolene, but Dad and Grandpa appeared with the cones and she could not continue. Dad kept up a discussion about Michael's science project all the way home.

Jolene tried to corner her brother before he entered the RV, but Dad's exclamation of "Chaos!" brought them both racing to the doorway. The dishes that Dad had left in the sink lay shattered on the floor. Papers and books, photos, the television remote, and the cell phone had been knocked to the ground. Michael's water bottle had tipped and water dripped from the computer's keyboard.

Jolene and Michael searched for Chaos. He was hiding beneath their father's bed, his eyes wide and round.

"That's it!" roared Dad. "From now on, when we go out, that creature needs to be locked up." His voice dropped as he struggled to control his temper. "This is three days in a row and just look at that keyboard."

Jolene couldn't imagine Chaos making this mess. The kitten had been exhausted from his explorations in 1913. And he never did this kind of thing when they were home. The mysteries of her life deepened.

Chapter fourteen

More restless than ever, Jolene wandered through the dim light of morning. She had already taken some leftovers to the dog. The hound trusted her now; today it had accepted the food from her hand. She was in no hurry to return to the RV. Dad had left early to photograph the sunrise, Grandpa was out for his usual walk and Michael had gone for a morning swim workout. Even Dave was already up, picking up garbage that had been strewn about the horseshoe pitch. "What happened?" she asked. "It wasn't the coonhound was it?"

A smile flickered across Dave's face. "I doubt if any dog could do this." He pointed towards the garbage receptacles, wire rectangular cages that enclosed metal trash cans. Despite the metal latch, one cage was open. "These vandals were wearing masks and striped tails."

"Raccoons?"

"Yep! The last owner had some trouble with them. They're very dexterous animals and like to get into the garbage — especially if there's fish in there."

"We had salmon a few nights ago," said Jolene, her eyes lighting up. "And we had trouble in the RV about the same time."

"They can unlatch doors and windows."

"But those were all closed when we returned," recalled Jolene. "The skydome!" The idea occurred to her at the moment she said it. "I'll look when I get home."

"Oh," added Dave, "tell your Dad that when you go to Sarnia, you're welcome to leave anything you don't want to take — bicycles, chairs, whatever — in the shed by the river. It's not locked and it's almost empty." He bent over to retrieve a wind-blown chip bag.

"I'll tell him," said Jolene. "Have you heard any more about the coonhound?"

"Just that they couldn't trap it. The animal services officer had to go out-of-town, but I expect he'll try again when he gets back." Dave inched his back upright. "I'd better contact him and have him bring a raccoon trap as well."

Jolene wondered if they'd kill the raccoon too. A sudden nausea rose from the pit of her stomach. "Are they planning to put the dog down when they trap it?"

"I haven't heard," he said, not unkindly.

"It's all because of that grizzly old guy!"

Dave's brow wrinkled. "Which old guy?"

"The one at the dock who got the crowd all fired up. He said he'd tell the animal services guys what had to be done."

Dave's teeth clenched momentarily. "That fella's name wouldn't happen to be Andy, would it?"

"Yeah! That's it. Why?"

Dave crumpled the chip bag. "We used to live beside Andy before we bought this place and I think it would be fair to say he dislikes dogs."

"Why?"

"A guard dog severed his Achilles tendon years ago," Dave replied. Jolene remembered the way Andy had limped along the dock. "He was trespassing on private property although he claims he never saw the signs." Dave sighed and Jolene recognized the look of a sad story. "It was because of Andy that we lost Ginger, our golden retriever." Dave's shoes scuffed the ground, as if he were digging for a memory. "Alice and I were both working and Andy, being a fisherman, was on his own schedule. He used to provoke Ginger until she barked, and then he'd file complaints. Eventually he convinced some of the other neighbours to complain and we were told we had to muzzle Ginger, get an electric collar or have her debarked." Dave's feet stopped, the memory unearthed. "We didn't have the heart to do any of those things, so we gave her away to a farm. I don't know if she's ever forgiven us."

Jolene's heart ached right alongside Dave's. "Couldn't you get her back now that you have this place?"

"We thought about that, but she's almost blind now and adapting to a new home would be hard on her."

"You could get another dog."

"We've thought about that too, but we'd need the right kind of pet here at the resort. A calm dog with an even temperament. A dog like Ginger," he added sadly.

"He had no right to do that!" declared Jolene, boiling at the unfairness of Andy's actions.

"Maybe not," agreed Dave, "but he did."

Pessimism overcame Jolene. If Andy hated animals that much, he'd find a way to have the coonhound put down. Hopelessness sunk deep inside her like a rock in a pond.

Jolene peered impatiently over Michael's shoulder at the computer monitor. She was feeling edgy, but it was not just because she had dreamed the highway dream again last night. Right now, she was anxious to return to the past and confront Em.

"You've spelled Harbor Beach the American way," she told Michael, pointing to a town on the shore of Lake Huron.

"That's because," retorted Michael, "it's on the American side." He shut down the computer.

Earlier, Grandpa had promised they could return to 1913 as soon as Michael was ready. Jolene was already changed and ready to go. While she waited for her brother to change,

Jolene twisted the pearly buttons of her dress. This morning, she had decided not to confide in Grandpa or Michael until she was sure. Sure that Em was actually Marissa Brighton from the present.

After hurrying along the trail and across the road, Jolene darted towards the station ahead of her brother and grandfather. She glanced down to ensure that Chaos was safely tucked inside her apron before entering the time crease. A warm breeze began to blow and her muscles grew tight. She closed her eyes against the pressure and felt herself being pulled apart before she was hurled into the past. This time there were no horses. A magpie squawked in disbelief, but nobody else registered her arrival at the station. Michael and Grandpa appeared moments later.

Leaving them at the harbour, Jolene climbed the hill to Em's place. Mary was in the backyard pinning up laundry, the wind teasing her braid. "Em's in the kitchen," she told Jolene. "Go on inside." Jolene dashed up the steps. At the back door, she hesitated. What was she going to say? She knocked timidly then let herself in.

Em looked distractedly away, composed herself and smiled graciously. "You're just in time to come mushroom picking." She handed Jolene a wicker basket. "We'll take the bicycles." Em avoided Jolene's eyes, but ran a hand over Chaos' soft head. "Why don't you leave him here?" she suggested. Jolene left Chaos sniffing about the kitchen and her hat hanging on a peg.

"Be careful," called Mary as the girls rode off on their bikes. Jolene's was basic black and felt oddly upright. Cycling towards Courthouse Square, Jolene wondered if Em would discuss the cell phone incident now that they were alone, but her friend said nothing. Studying Em as they rode, Jolene noted that the poster girl had a slightly plumper face, but that there were definite similarities. "Celeste got a letter from Edward. He's taken a berth on the *Wexford* with John. They'll both be here on Sunday."

"That's good news for Celeste," said Jolene.

Em rolled her eyes. "At least I'll miss their big reunion. Mary's sister in Sarnia broke her foot and she's got three small kids, so they're sending me to help out."

"I thought you hated little kids."

"I do, but the *Regina's* going to be there."

They had left the town behind. Small farms bordered the road and rows of tilled earth encircled stands of trees. The girls coasted down a hill and Em turned into the woods on a path buried in scarlet and gold. Ducking under a large oak tree, she dismounted and leaned her bike against the trunk. Jolene followed Em into the shadows of the forest. "We don't want the poisonous ones," she said lightly, "and any that are decaying we can forget about as well." She bent over a patch of mushrooms with brown stems and pink gills. "This is what we're looking for."

Small clusters were everywhere. Jolene squatted and plucked her first mushroom from its damp home. Her thoughts flitted back and forth between the past and present, but she wasn't sure how to broach the subject. Sunshine lanced the shadows and birds twittered. Giant oak leaves drifted to earth like unmanned parachutes.

Em wiped her muddy fingers on the grass. "When I'm older, I'm going to invent a mushroom-picking machine."

"In the future they'll have mushroom farms," replied Jolene, watching Em's delicate hands.

"Mmm," said Em, without looking up. "We could still do with some new inventions."

Em's comment triggered Jolene's thoughts. "George would be ecstatic with a digital camera," she said carefully, "and Celeste would love an electric hair dryer."

Em flashed a frightened look at her.

"And Mary could use a microwave."

Em jumped, upsetting her basket of mushrooms. She gave Jolene a wild sunflower stare. "What are you talking about?"

Jolene rose slowly to her feet, now certain that her hypothesis was correct. "The things they'll have in the twenty-first century, Em." She paused. "Or should I call you Marissa?"

Em's face paled and she began to sway.

Jolene put a hand out to steady her. "I'm from there too," she added quickly.

"You are? So how did you get here?"

"I came through a time crease. I'm guessing you did the same."

Em exhaled a long breath. "How would I know?" she said finally. "One day in August, I was just sitting on a bench in Goderich, looking at Frank's picture and I started feeling really weird — like someone was pulling my limbs apart. The next thing I knew I was in 1913 beside this old furniture factory near the Grand Trunk Railway Station." Her eyes were vast, like the ocean. "And then the factory went and caught on fire."

"That explains it," Jolene said excitedly. Em looked blankly at her. "A time crease always occurs near the site of a disaster."

Em stared incredulously, and Jolene was reminded of how skeptical she had been when Grandpa had first explained time creases to her. Em covered her face with her hands, and Jolene said nothing more, letting her friend digest her words. When Em finally looked up, her astonished look was fading. "So I came through a time crease." A smile inched up Em's cheeks. "It was the cell phone wasn't it? That's how you knew."

"And the pomegranate."

Em frowned. "But how did you know my real name?"

"We saw it on a missing persons poster in Goderich." Silence fell between them.

Squatting, Em began to gather her upset mushrooms. Jolene waited. "I ran away," Em said finally.

"Why?"

"Because I couldn't stand the thought of having to go to yet another foster home." Jolene could hear the bitterness in her friend's voice. Em hugged her knees in front of her. "My mother was an alien."

Jolene's mouth gaped. She lost her balance, landing on the grass beside Em. "An alien?"

"Yeah, you know — one of those people who enter Canada without all the right papers."

"Oh, you mean an illegal alien."

"Yeah. I was only three when she died. They gave me her papers — my birth certificate, her fake papers and that picture of Frank that I showed you."

"Did they try and find your father?"

"My father is listed as *unknown* on my birth certificate," replied Em. "So, I was put in the care of social services until they sorted things out — the first of many foster homes."

Jolene recalled the sweet little girl with the bewildered look she'd seen on the television. That had been Em, years ago. "Why weren't you adopted?"

"There was concern that some foreign relative might miraculously show up and claim me, so they didn't put me in the adoption pool until I was older. Most people want to adopt babies."

Jolene added a mushroom to her basket. No relative had come forward to claim Em. She wondered how Em's mother had come to possess Frank's photo, why she had kept a picture taken almost a century earlier, and if Frank was even a relative to Em. "Were they unkind at the foster homes?"

"Not all of them." Em sat in a reverie. "But I wasn't

exactly a model foster daughter either." Jolene made no comment and Em continued. "It happens. When nobody cares about what you do, sometimes you do stuff you shouldn't. Lots of stuff you shouldn't." Em's voice was contrite, but her expression was unrepentant. "Like steal a cell phone before you take off."

Jolene remained silent. It couldn't have been easy being shunted from one home to the next, but she'd seen first-hand that Em could be outspoken, opinionated and obstinate.

"So, I caught the train to Goderich, where that photo I showed you had been taken. I'm not sure why. The picture was from 1910 and I knew Frank would be long dead, but he was my only potential link to any real family."

"Couldn't you have tried to find out about him at the library?"

"I went there first, but they couldn't do anything without a last name." Em screwed up her face. "When I got to Goderich, I bought a slurpee and sat down on a bench in the shade. Then I pulled out the picture and started wondering what it would have been like to live in Goderich early in the twentieth century — as if I could just turn back the clock at that very spot."

"That's kind of how we time travel!" exclaimed Jolene. "You think of yourself as stationary letting time pass over you rather than travelling through time. That shadow must have been a time crease."

"Beats me!" said Em. "Next thing I knew I was in the midst of all this smoke and commotion. Everyone was running around wearing clothes that looked like they belonged in a museum. I found an old blanket and made myself a cloak to wear over my shorts and tank top."

"And then what did you do?"

"I hung around that burned-out building waiting for something to happen that would take me back to the present. But it never did."

"Weren't you scared?"

"Hungry. I must have looked pretty scary though because most of the women uptown avoided me. I found a bit of stale bread on one of the benches at Courthouse Square — I think it was meant for the birds." Jolene smiled sympathetically. "And then Mary saw me."

She stopped as if that explained everything and Jolene knew the rest. Mary had taken her home, taken her in, fed her, clothed her and eventually adopted her like a daughter. It was just like Mary.

"The name Marissa was too modern for 1913, so I decided to go by my initial, M." She twisted a lock of hair between her fingers. "And here I am, picking mushrooms and selling toffee, but I like it."

Jolene tried to fit together the new pieces of this puzzle. With no knowledge of time creases, Em had been stuck in the past, but there was no reason for her to remain now. "You can come back now, you know."

"Why would I want to?"

Jolene's mouth opened in an oval of surprise. "Don't you miss the present?"

"Oh sure. I miss my music, television and movies — those talking pictures are so primitive!" She caught her breath. "I miss taco chips, the internet, cars that go more than thirty kilometres per hour and salsa by the spoonful." Jolene wondered what she'd miss if she was suddenly separated from her family and life. "But I don't miss being passed from one home to the next with a file as thick as my hair." Em hurled a mushroom into the basket. "Besides, I might actually be able to find Frank here."

Jolene shifted to another patch of mushrooms, wrapping her fingers around the soft brown stems, and feeling the responsibility of this newly shared secret. They picked until their baskets were brimming. "Let's go home," suggested Em, making Jolene wonder if her choice of the word *home* had been deliberate.

Jolene's thoughts circulated in time with the wheels of her bicycle. What would she do if she were Em? Here, Em had a family who cared for her, and from what Jolene could tell, she cared for them, too. And there was always the chance that she'd meet Frank and find her real relatives.

"Can I watch?" asked Em as they parked their bikes behind the house.

"Watch?"

"You go through the time crease."

"I guess so," said Jolene. "You don't want to come back?"

Em cast a long look at the stone house with its copper turrets. "No!"

Leaving their baskets on the back stoop, the girls retrieved Chaos and walked to the park overlooking the elevators and the harbour. "The time crease is behind the railway station," said Jolene, pointing. "You'll be able to see us from here, but I'll have to find Gramps and Michael first."

"I'll wait," said Em. "Are you coming back?" she asked anxiously.

"Tomorrow morning. I promise." Jolene sauntered downhill, tucking Chaos into her hat and feeling Em's eyes on her. She found Grandpa and Michael conversing with a railway worker at the station. Together, the three of them ambled towards the time crease. Dad had planned on being back by suppertime and it wouldn't do to come parading into the RV in his museum exhibit clothes.

At the edge of the time crease, Jolene shaded her eyes with one hand and looked up to the hilltop. Em stood exactly where she had left her. Jolene waved and Em returned the gesture. Then, grabbing Grandpa and Michael's hands, Jolene sprang into the hot shadow and back to the present.

"Who were you waving at?" asked Michael after they'd returned. Grandpa also looked concerned.

"Em," replied Jolene. "Or should I say Marissa Brighton."

Michael stared at her in disbelief. "The missing girl?"

Jolene nodded. "That's Em," she said and she proceeded to tell her brother and grandfather the entire story.

"Wow!" Michael was amazed, as was Grandpa. They had arrived before Dad, and the twins were stuffing their clothes back into storage. "No wonder you thought there was something strange about her." Michael banged the door shut. "But I can't believe she doesn't want to come back. I mean being in the past is neat and everything, but doesn't she miss stuff."

"Salsa by the spoonful," repeated Jolene. "But I think she's happier in 1913."

"I wonder," mused Grandpa, chewing on the long hairs of his moustache, "if Em will change history if she stays in 1913?"

"But I thought you said we couldn't," challenged Jolene.

"Why is that anyway?" queried her brother.

"I don't know exactly," admitted Grandpa, "but your great-great grandfather noted the same thing in his journal."

"So why would Em be able to?" reiterated Michael.

"We only visit for a few days at a time. If Em stays in the past for many years, who knows what could happen. And there's always the possibility that she might change the history of the future."

"This is too complicated," said Michael. "I'm going for a swim. Maybe things will be clearer underwater."

"My brain hurts," moaned Jolene.

Grandpa rubbed her sagging shoulders, before asking her to do the impossible. "Try to forget about it for awhile."

Chapter fifteen

The persistent honking of Canadian geese filled the sky as Jolene strolled through the resort at dusk. A black hatchback, its hatch open, was parked in the ditch outside the hedge. Suspicion twisted into a hard knot in Jolene's stomach as the chiseled face of Andy came into view. Concealing herself behind the bushes, Jolene listened and watched as Andy held up a plastic-wrapped chuck of meat for his comrade to see. "Apparently they couldn't trap the beast, so I'm thinking it's time to take matters into my own hands." Andy flashed a caustic smile. "A little of this lying around should do the trick."

The colour drained from Jolene's face. Andy was planning to poison the dog. Bile rose in her throat and her emotions vacillated between fury and disgust. She heard the hatch thud shut and crept forward, following the grizzly old man, sticking close to the trees and, like the hound, staying in the shadows. On the trail that led to the marina, Andy raised his arm and tossed the meat into the woods. Only there wasn't just one piece as Jolene had thought; there were many smaller pieces. Hidden behind dense foliage in the dark woods, Jolene slumped to the ground as Andy's footsteps passed her. Now what was she going to do?

Think, she told herself. Stay calm and think. She'd never find all the chunks of poison meat before the dog did. But she might find the dog before it found them. Jolene hesitated. Would the hound come to her if she had no food? Whistling softly, Jolene strode into the forest. "Here boy," she called. A motion behind her made her heart jump with joy. She proffered her hand, partially closed as if she were concealing food. The dog's nostrils flared. It watched her warily. "Come on, boy," she urged. "You have to trust me."

As if it sensed the truth of her statement, the dog came to her. "Good dog." Sliding her belt free of her shorts, she looped it loosely around the dog's neck and led it unresistingly towards the bridge. The night sky offered them a protective quilt of darkness, studded with faint stars. Jolene paused at the bridge, her hands stroking the hound's smooth coat. Why would anyone want to kill such an innocent, gentle creature? Cautiously, they ventured across the deserted bridge into the resort. She had already decided where she would take the dog — the empty shed where Dave had offered to store their bikes.

The shed was within sight when Jolene heard the whir of an approaching bicycle. She broke into a run, crouching behind the shed and muzzling the dog gently with her hand as her father's voice faded. Aware that the moon was already hanging full and soft in the sky, Jolene eased the door of the shed open, leaving it ajar to admit a thin streak of light. Quickly, she blew aside abandoned spider webs, fashioned an old sheepskin jacket into a bed and slipped out the door to fill a child's sand bucket with water from a nearby tap. The dog eagerly lapped up the water, making Jolene wish she had food for the creature. At least here in the shed, it would be safe.

Running nimbly back to the RV site, Jolene knew that she needed an ally, an adult ally, but whom could she trust? Dad was already angry with Chaos, Grandpa had warned her to stay away from the coonhound, and she wasn't sure she could convince the resort manager that the dog was innocent.

"We were getting worried," Dad reprimanded her when she arrived. "It's already dark."

Jolene apologized, lowering her eyes to avoid Grandpa's inquisitive gaze.

"Chaos will be glad you're back," said Michael, trying to diffuse the tension. "He's ready for bed." The kitten was staring up at Jolene, yawning.

"At least he behaved himself today," added Dad, looking about the RV.

"It wasn't Chaos!" In all the excitement of the day, Jolene had completely forgotten about her earlier conversation with Dave.

"Jolene, we've been through all this before. Chaos was the only one here when the messes were made."

"It was a raccoon that came through the skydome," announced Jolene, praying that she was correct.

"Hmm," murmured her father skeptically.

"We could look," suggested Michael.

Taking a flashlight, Dad climbed the ladder to the top of the recreational vehicle. A network of tiny footprints covered the rooftop dust. "I don't believe it!" he exclaimed, holding up the dislodged wire screen of the skydome. "That raccoon's quite the burglar. It looks like I owe Chaos an apology."

Jolene didn't stay up to hear it. The evening had been a cacophony of emotions — the ascending roar of fury, the low persistent throb of trepidation, the delicate melody of relief. Now only the silence of exhaustion prevailed. She closed her eyes, confident that she would sleep tonight — right through the dream. And she did, but she didn't sleep through the short but passionate howls that came from the shed when the darkness of the night was the deepest.

Chapter sixteen

Jolene awakened with a clarity to her thoughts that had eluded her the previous night. Dad was still asleep and Grandpa gone for a walk when Jolene let herself out the door. Sunlight illuminated the filigree veins of a butterfly's wings and a fine mist hung in the air. Dewdrops clung to velvety flower petals, undisturbed by the passage of Jolene's decisive footsteps. While she was still uncertain that she could convince Dave of the dog's innocence, she was confident she could persuade him to believe in Andy's guilt.

She found the resort owner examining his garbage bins. One of the wire latches was undone, but the trash can was intact. "That dog howling last night must have scared that raccoon right off." He caught Jolene's eye. "You know anything about that?"

"Actually, I do," said Jolene, accepting his invitation to tell her story.

Dave grinned. "I suspected as much. You've been awfully interested in the fate of a certain coonhound." He settled his bulky frame on a picnic table and Jolene started at the beginning. She told him what had happened at the harbour and how Andy had been the one to suggest the dog be put down. She described the way fear had permeated the crowd, her encounters with the coonhound, and she confessed to setting off the trap. She repeated Andy's threats and told how she had stalked him into the woods, where he had thrown the poisoned meat amongst the trees. "I couldn't just leave the dog out there with the poison meat so I brought it here." Dave's eyebrows arched. "It's in your shed right now," confessed Jolene. "I didn't know what else to do."

Dave put a hand on her shoulder. "I'd say you've done just about as much as any one human could do for that dog," he said. "But I also think you did the right thing coming to me now. Poison meat in the woods is just plain dangerous." He rubbed his chin thoughtfully. "Are you around today?"

"This afternoon," replied Jolene, having promised Em she'd visit in the morning. Dad had arranged to have some diving equipment dropped off after two o'clock so they had to be back by then.

"Good," said Dave. "Leave things with me and I'll come find you later."

"What about the dog?" she asked meekly. "It hasn't been fed today and . . ."

"Have a look on the shelf at the back of the shed," said Dave. "One of our campers left a bag of dog food this summer."

Gratitude swept across Jolene. "Oh thank you," she whispered, throwing her arms around his neck.

Dave's big arms clumsily returned her hug. "And don't worry," he said, pulling his baseball cap down to hide his embarrassment. "I'll look in on the dog later this morning."

The coonhound greeted Jolene with eyes as bright and hopeful as her own. "Everything's going to be fine," she assured the gentle creature as it ate ravenously. Dave wouldn't let them down.

Back at the RV, Jolene unlatched the storage compartment and tugged at the box of clothing. Her delight in finding an ally for the dog had quickly been replaced by concern regarding Grandpa's news — the Great Storm would hit Lake Huron tomorrow in 1913. He had returned from his walk adamant that she try to convince Em to return to the present. His words echoed through her head. "Em belongs here, Jo, in the present. You have a responsibility to convince her to return." Jolene wasn't certain that she agreed with him, and she was even less certain that she would be able to do so.

Michael grabbed hold of the carton's stuck corner and

pulled. "Don't worry," he said as the box came free, "everything will work out."

"I don't see how I'm supposed to persuade her," Jolene complained. "She's so . . . well, Em's kind of like her hair."

"Half wild and untameable!"

"Yes!" It was a perfect description. "Even if she does come back now, what's to prevent her from returning to 1913 whenever she likes — the next time she runs away from a foster home?" Grandpa didn't understand.

Jolene's efforts to reason with her grandfather were in vain. By the time they had reached the time crease and returned to 1913, she was anxious to escape from his logic. Racing up the hill without waiting for Michael, she rehearsed the arguments she could use to persuade Em, but nothing felt right.

Her friend, dressed in a red dress with a lace collar, was sweeping the porch when she arrived. There was a briskness to her movements that Jolene noticed immediately. "William and I are leaving for Sarnia this afternoon and there's a lot to do." Em's hair was tied back in a ponytail, making her face seem longer and thinner than usual.

"We're driving there tomorrow morning," said Jolene.

"Really? Maybe we'll see you."

"We'll be almost a century ahead of you."

Mary barged through the door, her face flushed a bright red. "Good morning," she called, but Jolene noticed that she, too, seemed flustered. "Em, could you possibly deliver Mrs. Harper's toffee today? John and Edward will be here soon and . . ." She raised her eyes to the sky. "Lord, give me six hands and endless energy."

In the pantry, Em handed Jolene a basket of toffee. Then she shoved the pepper toffee that they had made into her apron. "Why don't we go by the school and see if we can't deliver these presents at the same time?" she said, letting out a witch-like cackle.

They crossed West Street and followed the ridge. While Em attempted to keep her hat on over her ponytail, Jolene sorted through her arguments, feeling uncomfortable and irritable. "So, have you thought about returning to the present?"

Em swung the basket. "I'm not leaving now when I'm this close to finding Frank."

"But he might not even be a relation!"

Life drained from Em's face. "The picture was with my mother's papers. He might be the only blood relative I'll ever know in my life."

"What if he isn't?"

"Then I'm a total orphan!" declared Em.

Jolene cringed. She hadn't meant to open up old wounds.

They had reached a castle-like house that overlooked the harbour. Em pulled a piece of toffee from the basket and tucked it in her apron before striding up the walk.

Two picket signs were firmly planted in the grass just outside the door. Pulling one free, Em held it high above her head. "Women deserve the vote!" she chanted, repeating the slogan on the placard and marching back down the walkway towards Jolene. "Mrs. Harper's a suffragette. She's been trying to get Celeste to go to a big convention in London."

"Will she go?"

"I doubt it. She's worried that they'll start burning houses and hurling hammers like they have in Britain." Em lowered the sign. "I'd go," she declared passionately, "even if it did get violent." Jolene frowned as Em marched back up the walkway, replanted the picket sign and knocked on the door. Violence didn't solve anything. It only made matters worse.

While Em delivered the toffee and chatted with Mrs. Harper about the suffragette movement, Jolene stared out at Lake Huron. The light in the dragon's eyes was twinkling. A sudden sense of foreboding filled the pit of her stomach.

"Aren't you tired of being Em instead of Marissa?" she asked when her friend rejoined her.

Em shook her mane of auburn hair. "No!" She clutched the handle of the basket as if hanging onto something she feared to lose. "I reinvented myself when I came here," she began. "I stopped stealing and cheating and lying because all of a sudden I didn't have to anymore. It was my choice to be someone else."

Jolene abandoned her attempts to persuade Em to return to the present, silently hoping that one day her friend would realize that Em could also be Marissa.

"My life hasn't been easy!" reiterated Em, oblivious to Jolene's thoughts.

Did hardship strengthen a person and spawn passion?

Grandpa had said that experiences played a big part in discovering passion, but he hadn't mentioned hardship. Jolene wondered if she would be stronger if she had been less fortunate.

They passed St. George's Anglican Church and turned left on North Street. Just ahead of them on the right was a two-storey brick building with a flat face and latticed windows. Jolene's feet stopped in their tracks. It was the Huron County Museum, only the sign above the door now read *Central School.* Children played tag outside on their recess break, their voices riding the wind.

"How come you don't go to school?" asked Jolene suddenly.

"I tried it for a couple of weeks, but I didn't like it."

Jolene was confused. Em was so convinced that Celeste should finish her medical degree, yet she couldn't see the value of an education for herself. "Didn't Mary want you to go?"

"Sure, but she couldn't force me to, could she?" Em transferred the special pepper toffee in her apron to the basket and placed the one she had removed from Mrs. Harper's pile on the top. Then she swung the basket on her arm as if silently summoning Simon and Harry. It worked.

"Look," called a familiar voice from a nearby tree, "it's the toffee girl." The boys were perched on a low branch above them.

"I didn't know rats could climb," Em said, stopping at the base of the tree trunk.

She set the basket down beside her and motioned to a little girl on the school field, who sprinted towards her. "Hi Em. Whacha' got?" The child's eyes darted to the basket and she licked her lips.

"Toffee," she said, holding up the piece she had pilfered from Mrs. Harper's order and passing it to her.

The little girl flashed her a grin missing two teeth. "Gee, thanks!" Then suddenly she cried, "Watch out!"

Jolene turned to see Harry with his knees wrapped around the branch. In one agile motion, he let go with his hands, swung down, grabbed the basket handle and lifted the entire batch of toffee into the tree. Above him, Simon lunged for the basket, applauding and hooting in delight.

"Give me back my toffee!" screamed Em. The boys greedily collected the remaining toffee, dropped the empty basket to the ground and stuck out their tongues at her. "Don't you dare eat those."

Simultaneously, the boys ripped open the wax paper. Opening their mouths as wide as they could, they bit into the sticky candy, chewing once then twice. "Ahhh!' screamed Simon, spitting the toffee to the ground. He fanned his mouth with a dirty hand. Harry's cheeks had turned bright red and his eyes watered. Their faces contorted into gruesome shapes, their tongues protruded from their mouths and Jolene thought she could see wisps of smoke coming from their ears. The girls bent their heads together, doubling over in laughter.

Behind them, Jolene heard a click and turned to see Michael, and George with his tripod and camera. "Perfect!" George declared, photographing the girls. He pointed the camera at the boys and took another picture.

"Now that's catching your subjects totally unaware," said Michael.

"Where were you?" asked Jolene.

"Photographing the interior of a church," said Michael, pointing at a nearby spire. "This is much more exciting."

"Water, water," begged Harry. The boys squirmed on the tree branch, debating whether or not to drop to the ground in front of the girls or suffer in the safety of the tree. Finally, Simon wiped his tongue on his shirt and Harry did the same. Below them, a growing group of children laughed and taunted.

With pangs in their ribs from laughing, Em and Jolene retrieved the basket and marched off towards Courthouse Square. George returned to the photography studio and Michael accompanied the girls. As the bells chimed, Em picked up the pace. "I'm packed, but I told Mary I'd help her bake if there was time."

Grandpa was sitting on the front porch beside the half-open door, reading a copy of the *Goderich Signal* newspaper. He looked up at his granddaughter, and Jolene averted her eyes. Em was not the persuadable sort. "I hear you're going to Sarnia this weekend," Grandpa said, addressing Em who had reached the bottom step.

"Actually," said Mary, coming to the door before Em

could respond, "William sent word that he's going to postpone his trip. The fellow that minds the shop for him when he's away is ill."

Disappointment flooded Em's eyes then quickly subsided. "Then I'll just take the train by myself."

"Oh no you won't!" Mary stepped onto the porch, a flour-streaked apron over her dress. "Not alone." Em opened her mouth to protest, but Mary wagged a plump finger at her. "You've never taken the train to Sarnia before and my sister can't meet you."

"I've travelled by myself lots of places."

Mary was resolute. "I don't care," she replied. "My bones feel like there's a storm brewing and I'll not have you gallivanting about on your own. William is going next week. You can go then."

"Next week?" Em looked crushed. "The *Regina* will be in Lake Superior by then."

"So be it," said Mary. "My sister will still have a broken foot and need help." Her eyes bored into Em and the girl turned meekly away. Mary disappeared inside, pulling the door shut behind her.

Em collapsed onto the stoop. "That's not fair," she said. "Doesn't she care about what I want? I have to get to Sarnia." Determination was creeping back into Em's voice. Jolene had a sudden vision of Em stealing away to the train station alone. It wouldn't be the first time.

Chapter seventeen

Jolene sat on the porch next to Em, a double-edged idea taking shape in her mind. "You could come to Sarnia with us tomorrow," she said carefully.

"In the present?" asked Em.

Jolene heard her heart patter as the plausibility of her plan registered. "Yes. We're driving down and Dad's going on a diving expedition."

Em looked thoughtful. "But then how would I get back to 1913 in Sarnia? Your time crease is here."

Grandpa's voice was low and even. "We came to Goderich because of the energy from the Great Storm."

A vague look of recollection crossed Em's face. "The Great Storm? I think we were supposed to read something about that in school once." She shrugged. "Was it this year?"

"It was," continued Grandpa, "and based on my knowledge and experience, I'd be very surprised if we didn't find time creases all along the shore."

"So we can go back once we're there?" Em's eyes glittered like sunlight on waves.

Grandpa's voice had an edge to it. "The closer we get to the actual event, the more dangerous it becomes."

"But we'll be okay on land," said Jolene quickly. The light in Em's eyes had started to fade.

"All we need to do is check out the *Regina* while it's docked," added Michael.

Jolene's thoughts were rapid as Grandpa played with his moustache, deliberating. She had persuaded her friend to return to the present, but not for the reasons Grandpa had voiced. Still, Jolene was betting that Grandpa would want Em back in the present even under those circumstances. She was right. Grandpa murmured his consent and Em jumped to her feet. "I have to tell Mary."

Within minutes, Mary had been convinced and the arrangements made. Em gathered her travel bag and coat. Mary gave Em a kiss and held her tightly. "Give my love to everyone. William will be there next week." She shook hands with Grandpa and hugged the twins.

Grandpa glanced at his watch as they headed down the hill. "We'll have to hurry if we're going to beat your father home."

"So what's a time crease look like?" asked Em.

"A hot shadow," Michael told her. "Just follow us."

At the station, Grandpa cut off the road to lead them around the back of it. Em slowed. "What if somebody in Goderich recognizes me?"

"They won't," said Jolene. "Just leave your hair down and you hardly look anything like the girl on the poster."

Em pulled the ribbon from her hair. She inched forward, then cast an anxious glance back up the hill. "What about everybody here?" she asked. "Will they be okay in the storm?"

Jolene took Em's hand. "You wouldn't be able to do anything anyway." She drew Em towards the time crease before she could follow Jolene's own troubled thoughts out to sea with John, Edward and all the other sailors steaming across the Great Lakes.

The shadow grew warm and the air become tangible. Em squeezed Jolene's hand and gasped. A gust of hot air hit them and Em bumped against her, her hat spiralling away. The pressure of the time crease weighed on their chests, stealing their breath in the darkness. Jolene concentrated on one location, letting time move past her. Then suddenly the time crease released them, hurling them forward into the light.

"What happened?" Em was pale and breathless.

"We're through," said Jolene, releasing her friend's hand. "Look!"

To their right stood the five massive elevators immersed in the buzzing and clanking of hydraulic machinery. The waters of Lake Huron rippled beyond the park and beach. "It's so green," said Em.

"It's September here," explained Jolene. "But time passes at the same rate in both places."

Em did some mental calculations. "I've been in Goderich just over two months."

"The same amount of time you've been gone from the present," Grandpa told her.

A minivan followed by a convertible drove up the hill. "Real cars!" exclaimed Em. "That's so cool." The wind gusted, ruffling the folds of their skirts. "What about our clothes?"

"Just look nonchalant and follow me," said Michael. "Once we cross the road, we're not likely to meet anyone else before we get home."

They navigated the walking trail behind the elevators, scurried across the road and entered the RV resort through the hole in the hedge. There was no sign of Dad and it was just as well. Not only would it have been awkward to explain their clothes, but it would have been almost impossible to account for all of Em's exclamations. "Television!" she declared entering the RV, "and a microwave and computer." She hugged the monitor.

"We better get changed," advised Grandpa. "Doug will be here shortly."

Jolene tossed Em a pair of shorts and a t-shirt and her friend disappeared inside the bathroom, muttering exclamations continually. Once they had stashed their 1913 clothes in storage, Jolene relaxed. Now Em was just a regular friend who had come for a sleepover.

The girls settled into the hammock with Jolene's discman, but before she could get too comfortable, she spotted Dave's burly form sauntering down the road in her direction. "I'll be right back," Jolene told Em, excusing herself.

Grandpa stood on the steps on the RV. "What's all this about?" Suspicion and concern mingled in his voice.

"The dog at the harbour," answered Jolene in a stoic voice. She needed to save her emotion.

"Maybe I ought to come along," insisted Grandpa, joining them.

Three men stood outside the resort office. Jolene recognized the tall fisherman whose son had dropped the cookie and the animal services officer she had lied to earlier, but she was unnerved by the sight of a policeman with a German shepherd sitting at his feet. Dave made the introductions while Grandpa's bewildered look intensified.

"Jolene is our guest who reported the distribution of the poison meat," explained Dave.

"Which," said the police officer reassuringly, "has all been cleaned up thanks to Mika's nose." The German shepherd turned her head at the mention of her name. "Obviously, it's illegal to leave poison in a public area and the perpetrator will be dealt with." He paused as Jolene's distress about her lies and trap-triggering increased. "Dave felt that it

would be best if you told us the rest of the story," he concluded. "He said he couldn't do justice to it the way you
could."

And so Jolene began at the beginning, again. The words
spilled out of her with an energy and intensity that she
hadn't known she possessed. They dispelled lies, begged
forgiveness and most importantly, pleaded for justice. The
men, including Grandpa, stood spellbound by her story.

"Well," said the policeman when she had finished, "I can
see why Dave thought we should hear it from you."

The fisherman agreed. "It certainly seems that I made an
incorrect assumption." He smiled apologetically. "My son
loves dogs. It's quite likely that he would have crawled right
underneath that pick-up truck and shared his cookie."

"So then," said the policeman addressing the animal services officer, "is there anything you'd like to see resolved?"

Jolene trembled. She had certainly broken the rules by
setting off the trap and harbouring a wanted stray dog. "As
far as I can tell, there's only the question of what to do
about that stray coonhound," he replied, winking at her.
Jolene's lips parted in a spontaneous smile, a sense of pride
infusing her entire being

"I guess you'll be looking for a home for the dog," said
Dave. "Unless you've managed to convince your father to
adopt it, Jolene."

Jolene coughed. The thought had never occurred to her.
The plight of the dog had moved her, but, she realized, the

desire to see justice served had been as important. She shook her head; Grandpa looked relieved.

"In that case," chimed Dave, "I've got raccoon trouble and I've been thinking that having a coonhound around here might be a good thing." Jolene almost jumped for joy.

"Now hang on a minute," replied the animal services officer, "we'd first need to see if it has a tattoo."

"It doesn't," replied Dave.

"I've already checked to see if there's been a hound matching that description reported lost and there hasn't been, but I'd recommend that you check the dog out first and see if you think it would be suitable for a resort like this."

"Done!" announced Dave. He reached behind him and opened the office door, whistling softly. The coonhound stepped outside, standing proud and alert on the porch. "There's no tattoo and he's been with us all day. Alice and I are convinced," he said, trailing his hands across the dog's back.

"Well then," said the policeman, "I guess our business here is finished."

Watching the men drive away, Jolene noticed that the colour of the sky had intensified in the last fifteen minutes, turning a clear azure blue. She stroked the dog's silky ears. "What are you going to call him?"

"Lucky," answered Dave. "Because he was a lucky animal to have met you when he did."

Jolene bent to give the hound a hug. After thanking Dave, she accompanied her grandfather back to the RV. He had been unusually silent through the whole scene. "Are you angry with me?" she asked.

Grandpa studied his granddaughter. "I'm exceptionally proud of you," he said finally. "I just wish I'd listened when you first told us your story." He paused. "But then I would have missed that impressive display of passion and determination."

Jolene grinned. A cricket chirped and a subtle breeze scalloped the clouds. Every sense felt as if it had suddenly awakened, every detail seemed more vivid and acute.

Grandpa spread his arms as if taking in the world. "If you care about rectifying injustice, then I don't suppose you'll ever run out of causes to inspire you."

Jolene appreciated her grandfather's insight. Following the road around the resort, she no longer doubted that she would find things in life to be passionate about. But those extraordinary events weren't common ones. It wasn't the same as having something to look forward to on a daily or weekly basis. It wasn't the same as having something tangible, like a sport, to call her own. Jolene sighed. Now that the initial euphoria had passed, she felt drained.

Chapter eighteen

Jolene joined Em in the hammock, where modern music had suddenly become the best thing since toffee. Their ears were still attached to the headphones when Dad arrived. "Hello everyone," he called. "Oh, hello," he said, catching sight of Em.

Jolene tugged the headphone from her ear. "Dad, this is Em," she said, trying to sound nonchalant. "She's come for a sleepover tonight."

Dad's face fell. "Oh, Jolene, we have to be in Sarnia first thing tomorrow."

"A sleepover with a road trip," Grandpa cut in. "I bet you've never done that before, Em."

"Nope," said Em. "I'm looking forward to it."

Dad looked uncertain. "I guess it's all right as long as your parents are okay with this."

"I spoke to her mother personally," Grandpa told him.

"Good." Dad seemed more at ease. "We're headed to Sarnia early tomorrow but you three won't have to get up. Jolene and Michael's grandfather will drive you back to Goderich that same day."

"Sounds cool," Em assured him.

Michael stepped out of the RV wearing his swim trunks. "Darn," he said, catching sight of his father. "I was hoping you were the guy with the drysuits."

"Sorry to disappoint you," said Dad, entering the RV.

"Anybody coming to the pool?" asked Michael, winding his towel around his forearm.

"I wish," groaned Em. "But I don't have my swimsuit."

"I have one you can borrow," said Jolene. "Only it's a bit old."

"That's okay. The last one I had was really old. It covered my entire body and had stockings with long pantaloons and an overskirt." She glanced at Michael. "Maybe you could teach me swim," she suggested.

"Sure," he agreed. "Let's go."

They changed and made their way to the pool. Impulsively, Jolene dropped her towel and dove into the glittering water. She hit the water with a loud splash. She swam to the edge, hauled herself out of the water and dove again. This time she kept her body tight and streamlined, noting that her entry into the water was much cleaner and quieter.

Em eased herself cautiously into the water and Michael swam to her side, eager to begin lessons. "Okay," said Michael, "the first thing is to get your head wet." Watching Em laughing and sputtering, Jolene wondered if she would still want to leave.

"How's the swim lesson going?" Grandpa inquired, arriving at the pool as Em pulled herself to the edge.

"There's a reason I don't have gills or flippers."

Michael laughed. "She's doing fine." He turned and swam butterfly with a strong dolphin kick.

"Oh sure, make me feel good," Em cried after him. She settled herself on a towel in the sunshine. "This is so nice."

"Not much sun tanning in 1913?" asked Grandpa.

"Not in those awful bathing suits," admitted Em, "and Celeste would have killed me if I had — all those horrible freckles and wrinkles." She tilted her head and watched Michael do a length of breaststroke. "She'll be in a frenzy right now, knowing that Edward's on his way."

Jolene said nothing. Edward, she knew, was on board the *Wexford*, along with John. Today was Saturday. The storm would hit Lake Huron tomorrow. She'd have to ask Michael what had happened to the ship during the storm — when Em wasn't around.

"Your dad sent me to tell you that supper will be ready shortly," said Grandpa.

They could smell steak grilling as they neared the RV.

Dad had barbequed, baked potatoes and concocted two salads for dinner. They ate outside on the picnic table with Chaos perched on Jolene's lap demanding scraps of steak, which discreetly found their way to him.

After supper, Dad plugged his cell phone in to recharge. "Don't let me forget this in the morning," he said, continuing his preparations for the next day.

The sun, a mango-coloured orb, sank until its rays gilded the hilltop. "Let's go watch the sunset at the marina," Grandpa suggested.

"I'll just tell Dave we're stepping out for a bit," Dad said, "in case the dive equipment arrives while we're gone." Grabbing his camera, he hustled towards the office.

On their way to the marina, Jolene stopped halfway across the Maitland River bridge, detaining Em. "Have you changed your mind?" she asked her friend. "About staying in the past?"

Em sighed. "I'll come back to the present some day," she admitted. "I never realized how much I missed the twenty-first century. But right now, I still feel as if there are things I need to do in 1913."

"Gramps believes that we can't make any significant changes to history," Jolene said tentatively. "You might not be able to either." Jolene wondered what would happen if Em found her family or met someone and fell in love.

Em shrugged. "That's okay. Women will get the vote with or without me. I just want to be a part of it." Her voice softened. "These last two months — being part of a family even if they haven't been my real family — have been pretty special. Even if it doesn't last forever, the memories will."

Jolene smiled at her friend. The present was still changeable and perhaps Em's experience in the past would ultimately shape her future and her ability to be a new Marissa.

"One day," said Em as if she'd read Jolene's mind, "I'd like to be a social worker."

"You'd have to go back to school," advised Jolene.

"I know," said Em grimacing, "but then there'd be a reason to." She tugged at Jolene's sleeve. "Come on. Let's catch up."

The girls joined Michael and Grandpa at the end of the pier, and Dad arrived moments later. The sun was dropping, its orange rays diffusing into streaks. Standing between Grandpa and Em, Jolene felt an uneasiness growing inside her. Em had accompanied them to the present believing that Grandpa would allow her to pass through a time crease in Sarnia to 1913. The fiery ball of sun sank towards the horizon. But Jolene doubted if Grandpa had any intention of permitting Em to time travel in Sarnia so close to the Great Storm — an easy thing to do since he alone was able to find the time creases.

The shimmering orb reached the blue edge of the water and began to lose its symmetry. Grandpa had been adamant that Em belonged in the present, almost as adamant as Em had been about remaining in the past. Watching the sky, awash in pinks, reds and oranges, Jolene wondered whose passion would win out.

Chapter nineteen

E m murmured in her sleep and Jolene woke as the RV
slowed. "Are we there?" she whispered down to her
grandfather seated in the passenger seat.

"We're at Bright's Grove, about ten minutes north of
Sarnia."

Their voices woke both Michael and Em, and by the time
Dad pulled into the marina, all three children were up. "Put
your swimsuits on," he suggested. "There's a nice beach here."

"And I want to try a drysuit," said Michael eagerly. "I've
heard they squeeze your skin so tight that you stay perfectly
dry." The drysuits had been delivered to the resort while

they were watching the sunset last night, and since Dave hadn't known how many of them were diving, he'd advised the man to leave four suits.

"As long as Gramps doesn't mind hanging out here for awhile," said Dad.

"Not at all," said Grandpa. "I might find some good stories."

The girls pulled shorts and a t-shirt over top of their swimsuits, knowing that the sun still had some work to do that morning.

The dock was a flurry of activity. Boats of all shapes and sizes came and went. Dad located the diving expedition and selected a drysuit. Jolene and Michael helped him transfer his gear to the dive boat. After hugging them both, Dad stepped on board, his excitement growing like the heat of the day. They watched as the captain manoeuvred the boat out of the slip and into the St. Clair River. Dad stood at the railing, one hand raised in farewell.

"I'm putting on a drysuit and jumping in the lake," said Michael, pointing at the RV where the rest of the diving suits had been left.

While Grandpa wandered among the boats, Michael chose a leathery, black suit, stripped down to his swimsuit, and squirmed into it. Jolene and Em watched him for a moment and then did the same, surprised at how tight the diving suits were and how warm. The diving suits covered their entire bodies from their necks to their ankles to their wrists. Only their hands and faces remained uncovered when they pulled up their hoods. "Let's go show Gramps," Michael said, loping along the pier. Grandpa did not notice them approach. He was standing beside an unmanned life-guard station, staring out at the lake.

"Hey Gramps. We're going in," called Michael.

Grandpa remained mesmerized.

"Gramps?"

"What's wrong with him?" asked Em.

Jolene had seen that look in her grandfather's eyes before. "He's found a window."

"Into the past," her brother explained.

"Is that the same as a time crease?" asked Em.

"Yes," Jolene confirmed. "Only he's elected to look through it instead of step into it." Jolene had seen windows into the past before — once in a coal mine and once in Halifax.

They pressed forward, following Grandpa's gaze. A warm breeze caressed their faces and Jolene saw a large iron freighter at the dockside. Men, dressed in fur-trimmed coats, fought the wind as they waited to unslip the heavy ropes that secured the ship.

"It's the *Regina*," gasped Em, reading the ship's name on the hull.

Jolene gripped Em's arm with one hand and Grandpa's with the other. "Gramps," she said, shaking him. He swayed unsteadily then looked at them as if seeing them for the first time that day.

"I'm going back," announced Em, "through the time crease."

"No, you're not," said Grandpa, quickly recovering.

"But it looks like the ship's almost ready to sail," insisted Em. She softened her voice. "I just want to talk to the sailors and see if Frank is on board. Please."

Jolene caught Grandpa's eye. Now that Em knew the location of the time crease, there was little he could do to prevent her from returning. Jolene was betting that he'd prefer to go with Em rather than let her return alone. His moustache twitched, but he conceded. "All right, but first we need to change."

They ran back to the RV. "Just throw your clothes over top of the drysuit," said Em as they pulled the clothing from the box. Jolene and Michael did so, smoothing one another's garments over their compact drysuit hoods. Chaos swatted at the cord of Dad's forgotten cell phone sending it clattering to the floor, and then sneezed. Jolene patted his little head before dropping her hat and racing back to the dock.

Rushing towards the lifeguard station, they ignored the surprised looks of a small group of tourists they passed. At the lifeguard station, Jolene felt the shade tingle and reached for Em's arm. Her body stretched and strained against the drysuit and she felt as if she would suffocate. A blast of hot air hit her, followed by a cold gust of wind. The lifeguard station had been replaced by a decrepit wooden shed. Sarnia in 1913 stretched along the shore of the river.

"There she is," cried Em. "The *Regina*."

Grandpa stepped in front of them, blocking their way. "Your feet may not leave the pier," he told them sternly. "Understand?"

The children nodded mutely. They all hurried towards the freighter. Inky smoke spewed from its large smokestack. Rectangular wooden hatch covers spanned the deck and on top of these stood an ominous stack of iron pipe.

"She's a straight decker," said Michael.

Grandpa pointed to the bow. "Her pilothouse is built forward and her engine room is in the rear. There's a continuous cargo hold in between." A frown sobered his features. "She's sure loaded top-heavy though. That pipe on deck will make her awfully unstable."

They had reached the stern and the oily stench of the smokestack. "That's the boiler room below the iron grates," explained Grandpa, securing his hat against the wind. "That way there's always fresh air to feed the fires." He pointed at a large rectangular building in the stern. "And that houses the kitchen or galley and the afthouse, where the crew bunks."

Em pressed through the crowd until they had reached the midpoint of the ship. Jolene could see the pilothouse in the bow atop the captain's and officers' quarters. Two narrow ladders led up to it and donut-shaped life preservers were secured to the railing outside. A long steering pole protruded from the bow of the ship. Jolene was glad of the drysuit beneath her clothes, for the wind had a bite to it.

Grandpa stayed close by, greeting the sailors and stevedores who stood in small groups, pulling up their collars against the wind and smoking to keep warm. At the edge of the harbour, the water peaked in whitecaps and snowflakes began to swirl.

"It's crazy setting out in this," said one sailor, his cap pulled low over his eyes.

An older unshaven man exhaled a column of grey smoke. "Captain McCallum's a good man and the *Regina's* a good ship. He wouldn't put us out in anything we couldn't handle."

"What's the word from the weather bureau, Frederick?" asked another.

"Storm warning's up," replied the seasoned sailor. He indicated a series of flags on a nearby pole — a white pennant above a red flag with a black square centre. "But then it's been up for two days already."

"Is that the signal for a hurricane?" Jolene whispered to Michael.

Michael shook his head. "There isn't one."

"I've seen worse on these waters and lived to tell about them," continued Frederick. He stroked the grey stubble on his cheeks. "Besides, this will be my last trip up the lakes so it's only fitting that it be a memorable one."

"You're retiring?" asked his shipmate.

"Moving out to Saskatchewan. My sister's out there now."

"I hear their lakes are the size of our puddles," said a voice in the crowd.

Em hovered on the edge of the laughing men with Grandpa at her elbow. "Excuse me," she said, digging her photo out of her pouch, which hung around her neck. "I was wondering if you can tell me if this man, Frank, is on board the *Regina*. He's a relative."

Frederick took the photo from her. "Why he certainly is," he said. Em's eyes sparkled. "That's Frank Silver, our new engineer. Just came over a few weeks ago."

"Can I see him, please?"

"I expect he'll be busy getting ready to set out," said Frederick, "but perhaps he could find a minute to step ashore."

"I'll pass on the message," said the man who had first protested about sailing in poor weather. He strode up the ramp onto the boat.

Em fought bravely to hide her nervousness. She fidgeted with the picture, transferring it from one hand to the other.

Jolene squeezed her forearm and Grandpa stayed close to Em's side. Activities aboard the ship and on the dock continued. "Where is he?" murmured Em when the sailor did not reappear.

A few sailors rechecked the pipes that had been lashed to the deck. Grandpa chatted to Frederick, one of the *Regina's* mates, amidst the organized confusion of a ship about to set sail. Em grew more and more impatient with each passing moment.

Finally, Frederick took his leave of Grandpa and climbed

aboard. "Where is he?" reiterated Em, exasperated. Whistles blew and the men shifted in anticipation. An angry gust of wind sent Grandpa's hat bouncing down the pier. He chased after it as it rolled and skidded across the wooden planks. Seeing her chance, Em dashed up the ramp onto the ship. Panic struck Jolene. "Em!" she screamed over the noise.

"What's she doing?" demanded Michael.

"The ship's setting sail!" proclaimed Jolene. The twins exchanged desperate looks.

"She'll be headed to the boiler room," shouted Michael.

"Come on. We'll have time to find her!" Jolene darted up the ramp with Michael close behind her.

Quickly, they manoeuvred along the ship's deck towards the stern, banging into astonished sailors and equipment while they searched for Em. She was nowhere in the vicinity of the boiler room. Jolene continued her search, calling frantically for her friend. She slipped on the wet deck boards and struggled to her feet.

"Jo! Jo!" She looked up at the sound of Michael's voice, suddenly aware of the motion of the boat. The dock was slipping past her.

"Michael," she cried, catching sight of her brother.

He stumbled towards her. "We have to get off."

"What about Em?"

Michael's response was drowned out by the blast of a whistle. The boat pulled farther away from the pier. The twins made their way to the stern and looked back through the skeins of snow. Grandpa was standing on the wharf, gesturing frantically at them. "Jump," he screamed in a voice filled with terror.

Em joined them at the railing. "We have to jump!" screamed Jolene.

"But I can't swim," protested Em. She backed away from the edge of the boat then turned and ran towards the pilot-house. "I'll make the captain stop."

Grandpa's figure was becoming blurry. Michael gripped Jolene's hand. "I think we should jump."

Jolene turned to watch Em. "We can't, Michael. We can't leave her." Side by side, they stood watching until Grandpa's outline was no longer visible.

"Hey, what's this?" asked Frederick, coming upon them.

"Em went looking for the engineer," explained Jolene, "and then the boat set sail. Michael wanted to swim for it, but Em can't swim." Her voice cracked with emotion.

"There, there," said Frederick. "That water's mighty cold. I wouldn't advise a swim anyway." Jolene wondered how much protection their drysuits would offer them. "Everything will be just fine," continued Frederick. "This here's a package freighter. She stops all the way up the lake. We'll put you off first stop and make sure you get home." He patted Jolene's hand. "Come along now and meet the captain and a few of the crew. I don't suppose you've ever been on a freighter like this before."

Em was already in the pilothouse when Jolene and Michael arrived. The tiny D-shaped room had large windows around the curved front and on each side. Smaller windows looked back at the stern. A chart table stood along the back wall and in the middle of the room was a compass binnacle and a steering wheel. A red-haired wheelsman stood behind it guiding the boat up the mouth of the St. Clair River into Lake Huron while another officer stood watch. Captain McCallum, seated on a stool in front of the wheel, gave them a good-natured grin. "These must be Jo and Michael," he said to Frederick. "We've already met Em." The tone of his voice said more than his words. He rose to his feet. "I'm Captain McCallum and this is my wheelsman, and my first mate."

The wheelsman did not take his eyes off the channel. The first mate tipped his cap to them with a sinewy hand. "It's not every day that we have stowaways," he said.

"We're not stowaways," declared Em, eliciting a bemused smile from the captain.

"You'd best take our guests down to the officers' quarters while we're navigating the river," the captain told Frederick.

Michael's stomach rumbled loudly and Frederick laughed. "I'll do that," he said, "but first I think we ought to visit the galley."

Together they walked the length of the boat and entered the ship's kitchen. The cook was as good-natured as the captain and soon all three children were enjoying a meal of milk, pancakes and thick butter. Frederick left them with instructions to come find him in the pilothouse when they were done.

While the cook bustled about the kitchen, Michael interrogated Em. "Where did you go? We went straight to the boiler room and couldn't find you."

"I thought engineers drove the ships," explained Em, "not ran the boilers." She grinned sheepishly. "Did you see Frank?"

"No, everyone was busy," replied Michael.

Jolene turned anxious eyes to her brother. "What are we going to do?"

"We're going to get off at the first stop."

Em stabbed a pile of pancakes. "What's the big rush? I haven't seen Frank yet."

Jolene set her fork down noiselessly. She hardly dared ask the question that lay on her lips, but she summoned her nerve. "Michael, what happened to the *Regina* in the storm?"

Chapter twenty

Michael set his glass of milk down, his eyes reflecting the anxiety in Jolene's. "I don't know what happened to the *Regina*, Jo. I'm not that far in my project yet."

"What are you talking about?" interrupted Em.

Jolene took a deep breath. "The Great Storm is due to hit Lake Huron today," she said, lowering her voice and eyeing the cook.

Em's fork clattered to the table. "Today?" Panic turned her eyes a crystal blue. "Did the *Regina* sink?"

"We don't know," said Michael.

"Well, let's ask someone," sputtered Em. Jolene arched one eyebrow and Em squirmed. "Okay, so let's do something else."

"Like get off at the first stop," reiterated Michael.

"The weather wasn't too bad when we boarded," Jolene said slowly. "Do you remember when the storm hit?"

"In the afternoon."

"So the plan is to find Frank and be ashore by then, right?" asked Em.

"Hopefully," said Michael. "I don't know where the first stop is, but I bet Frederick does."

They left their half-eaten meals, thanked the cook and made their way back onto the deck. Leaden clouds pressed down on grey-green waves. The wind was still gusting and the snow spinning. Jolene noticed the crew stringing a wire from the bow to the stern on the main deck. "It's a jackline," explained one of the sailors. "Sometimes the winds get so fierce and the decks ice up so bad, we can't get from one end to the other without it."

Jolene heard Em gulp behind her. She swallowed the lump in her own throat and followed Michael towards the pilothouse. Frederick intercepted them at the door of the officers' quarters and waved them inside. Bunks lined the walls next to a few worn armchairs. Michael, Jolene and Em perched on the beds.

"So did you quiet your stomachs?" asked Frederick.

"Yes, thank you," said Jolene. Had the *Regina* sunk during the storm?

The question weighed so heavily on them that even Frederick felt it. "So what's the problem now then?"

Michael spoke. "Where's the *Regina* going?"

"We're headed to Fort William."

"Thunder Bay," whispered Michael, letting Jolene and Em know the name of the city in the present.

"Could we just make a quick stop at Goderich first?" asked Em.

Frederick chuckled. "That'd be quite the detour," he said, "since we'll be navigating along the American coast." He leaned back in his chair. "We're more likely to stop at Harbor Beach and at some of the other lake communities that depend on us for their winter supplies. We're carrying everything from hay and pipes to razors and champagne."

Jolene attempted a smile. "How long will it take to reach Harbor Beach?"

"Depends on the winds," replied Frederick. "Normally it's a five-hour trip, but with the wind coming out of the west like this, it could take longer."

Jolene did some mental calculations. They had left around seven-thirty this morning. That meant that they would reach Harbor Beach sometime in the early afternoon.

"Can't we go any faster?" asked Em.

Frederick gave her a curious smile. "Are you wanting to stoke the boilers yourself, miss?"

"No," admitted Em, "although I would like to meet Frank."

"He'll be awful busy at the moment. Relax for a bit."

"I can't," muttered Em, "not in this weather."

"Ah, so that's it," said Frederick. "You needn't fear. The captain's a solid seaman."

"What about the storm warning flags?" asked Em. "He didn't pay any attention to those."

"Those flags have been flying for two days now," Frederick told them. "Most storms on the Great Lakes blow themselves out in three. Besides, there isn't a captain on these waters who pays much heed to those signals."

"But why?" asked Michael. "I thought they were issued by the weather bureau."

"They are," said Frederick, "but if we stayed in port every time there was a storm warning, we'd lose dozens of sailing days every year. Most of the captains I know would rather depend on their barometer and experience." He rose. "I'm going to get a cup of tea from the galley. Why don't you go up and visit Captain McCallum. He's a family man and I expect he'll be happy to have you in the pilothouse now that we're out of the river."

"Could you take me to see Frank?" asked Em.

"I've asked him to come up when he's done his shift, miss." Frederick's voice was stern. "We've got a long trip ahead of us."

Jolene, Em and Michael remained huddled together on the hard bunk after Frederick had left. "With any luck we'll be on shore in five or six hours," observed Jolene. "Then we'll just have to figure out how to get back to Goderich from wherever we are."

"I don't care," said Em, "as long as we're on land. I'm already starting to feel seasick."

They made their way up to the pilothouse where Captain

McCallum was poring over his charts. Jolene stared silently out the windows at the white peaks and rolling seas, but Michael's curiosity soon got the best of him. "Do you have a depth sounder?" he asked.

"We do," replied the captain. "We use it to measure the depth of the water so that we know how far off the coast we are. Generally speaking, we don't have to deviate very far from the American shore."

The thought reassured Jolene.

"What's this?" asked Em, pointing at a long calibrated glass tube mounted on a piece of wood.

The captain lifted his hat, which was hanging over the top of it. "Our barometer. It measures the air pressure, which is a pretty good indication of the weather."

"Isn't it kind of low?" asked Michael, looking at the mercury.

"It's a little lower than we'd like," admitted Captain McCallum, "but the direction it's moving is actually more important than the reading."

"What's happened since we left?" asked the wheelsman.

"It's low but steady." The captain re-covered it with his hat, making Jolene wonder if he couldn't find a more suitable hanger. A gust of wind hit the pilothouse and the wheelsman fought to steady the boat. "And we have a wind vane," said the captain, "but it doesn't tell us the velocity. I'm guessing from the sound that it would be about thirty miles per hour with higher gusts."

Michael inched his drysuit back to glimpse his Ironman

watch. It was quarter past ten. He settled himself beside a window and watched the tumultuous waves. Jolene did the same, but the intensity of the water frightened her.

"Are we there yet?" asked Em, after a brief silence.

The captain laughed as Frederick blew into the pilothouse, the wind banging the door shut behind him. "Quite the gale," he said. He glanced at the children. "Cook said to tell you that he's making biscuits for lunch and could use a few extra pairs of hands if you're willing."

"Sure," said Em. "Come on, Jo." Jolene joined her at the door. Michael, she knew, would stay in the pilothouse.

"Bring us back some warm rolls, won't you?" said Frederick.

Jolene and Em ducked through the door and climbed down the ladder. The wind whipped their skirts and drove the snow into them. Em set foot on deck and was blown sideways almost immediately. Clutching one another's hands, they fought their way to the galley and descended into its cozy warmth.

Jolene was grateful to have a distraction, and the cook was grateful to have the help. Em was an expert, quickly kneading and rolling out the bread as she had done for Mary many times in the past few months. Jolene followed her example and the galley soon filled with the aroma of fresh-baked buns. While the cook dished out lunch, Jolene and Em wrapped some warm rolls in a napkin and made their way back on deck.

The wind whistled fiercely and the girls bent low into it,

trying to keep their balance. A sailor gestured to them, indicating the wire stretched alongside the ship. "Hold onto the jackline," hollered Jolene, but the wind swept her voice away. She tugged at Em's dress. They groped their way along the jackline to the bow of the boat, the wind driving the snow into them. Despite the fact that their dresses and hair were wet, they were dry beneath their drysuits.

"It's cold," said Michael disappointingly when Em handed him a roll.

"Yeah, well the delivery truck stalled on account of the weather," Em told him. She distributed the rest of the buns.

The wheelsman was still at the wheel and did not relinquish his grip. Frederick, who had replaced the first mate, took his roll but did not eat. Jolene glanced nervously around the small room. "The wind seems to have picked up," she said. "And it feels colder."

The captain did not reply. He stared out the windows, searching for landmarks and speaking in hushed tones to Frederick, while Em, Jolene and Michael munched on their bread.

"What's happening to the barometer?" Jolene whispered to Michael.

"It's dropping."

"Why do I get the feeling that's not good?" moaned Em.

The waves were certainly not dropping. Jolene watched as walls of water broke across the stern of the ship. She said a silent prayer of thanks that the hatch covers had been properly secured. "Are we close to Harbor Beach yet?" she whispered to her brother.

He shrugged. "Even the captain's not sure. It's getting harder and harder to pick out landmarks in this blizzard."

Suddenly, the ship reeled, rocking from one side to the other and dipping down into a trough before climbing out of it again. Em set her bun down and covered her mouth. "Oh oh," she said, "I think I'm going to be sick."

"Why don't you girls go down to my quarters," suggested the captain. Although it was phrased as an invitation, it sounded like an order.

Jolene and Em dutifully obeyed. They made their way to the captain's small suite of rooms. Em headed directly for the washroom and Jolene could hear her retching and vomiting. Jolene paced about the rooms, looking out the partially snow-covered windows. Occasionally, she spotted a crew member struggling against the elements on the main deck, but soon it seemed as if every wave swept the deck clear. The men remained in the afthouse. Em emerged from the washroom looking slightly less green. She lay on the bunk, ill and groaning.

Heavy snow clouds battered the lake as the *Regina* smashed headlong into the mountainous seas. Em drifted off to sleep and Jolene shut her eyes and ears against the seething waters and wailing winds. Finally, around three o'clock, Michael stumbled into the suite. "What's it like up there?" asked Jolene.

"Not good, Jo." Fear prickled his voice.

"I'm going up," said his sister. Michael followed her back up the narrow ladder and into the pilothouse. Frederick and the captain were studying the charts. Colossal waves continued to march down the lake, creating deep troughs that the *Regina* crashed into and climbed out of again and again. Every time the ship went into a trough, Jolene felt the captain urge it forward, as if his willpower could somehow pull it through the dangerous seas.

Blinding snow now whirled in a crazed manner, reducing visibility to almost nothing and coating the windows with ice. "Come on, come on," muttered Frederick. "There ought to be a lightship or a lighthouse or the shore lights." But no lights glimmered in front of the boat.

Jolene turned frightened eyes on her brother. They should be near Harbor Beach by now, but how would they find it if there were no lights visible? The non-stop thunder of the waves tumbling and crashing mixed with the high-pitched whistle of the wind in the rigging lines. Jolene turned away, glancing out through the tiny windows toward the stern. A figure seemed to be moving along the main deck, harnessed to the jackline. "Who's that?" she asked.

The captain met the man at the door of the pilothouse, pulling him out of the wind tunnel into the light. At that moment, a gigantic wave roared over the roof, ripping the window shutters free. The wind pursued it, causing the battered windows to rattle and moan.

The man leaned against the door, catching his breath. "Frank sent me, Captain," he said. "The grates above the boilers are iced over and the engine room's swamped. He doesn't know how much longer he'll be able to keep her at this speed, sir."

The captain stood, his spine rigid. "Tell him we're going to come around," he said, his voice bold and deliberate. "We'll make a run back down to the St. Clair River. It'll be risky trying to find the mouth of the river, but it can't be worse than this."

"Can't we make Harbor Beach?" asked Jolene. Fear was beginning to squeeze her heart.

"Not in these conditions," said the captain. "Tell Frank that I'll need every bit of power he can coax from the boilers," he told the sopping crewman. "We've got to bring her around without letting her stay in the trough too long."

Jolene remembered the load of pipe on deck. Grandpa had said it would make the ship unstable, and now the captain wanted to turn in these seas. A wave much higher than the boat sent the captain's stool clattering across the room. Jolene lost her balance and grabbed for Michael.

"You children go down to my cabin," ordered the captain. Jolene studied his dark eyes but could detect no fear. She hurried past him and followed Michael outside. Water washed into the pilothouse and she clung to the ladder's railing.

Inside the captain's quarters, they found Em lying on the

bunk, staring at the ceiling. "What's happening?" she asked as they entered.

"The captain's decided to come around and head back to the south end of the lake." Dread coated Jolene's words and she did not look at Em. She peered out the ice-rimmed windows, straining to see the crew member who was bravely attempting to return to the boiler room.

"Isn't that dangerous?" asked Em, sitting up.

Michael nodded. "We have to turn sideways to the waves," he explained. "If we get stuck in a trough, the boat could be swamped and we'd capsize." He glanced up at Jolene. "Then the dragon wins."

Jolene lowered herself onto the bunk beside Em, remembering Mr. Clarkson's words. The dragon had unleashed its violent wrath on them. Now they were going to turn and try to flee. Jolene wondered how the dragon would respond.

Seated in the captain's quarters, Jolene felt the dark quiet reach out and stroke her spine. The children waited, their senses on full alert. After what seemed like an eternity, they felt the ship's bow change direction. The ship was coming around. The wind shrieked and the waves rammed the door. Their heartbeats pounded inside the cabin. The *Regina* dropped into a deep trough, rolling heavily from side to side. Mountain-high seas smashed over her and she wallowed in the trough. Jolene fell off the bunk and tumbled against the wall. Em was flung against her and they lay on the floor as the boat rocked and reeled. Finally, Jolene felt the freighter right itself and begin to climb out. She and Em dragged themselves back to the bunk.

"I think we made it," said Michael. "Now we'll have the wind behind us. It won't take long to reach the river."

But the boat still lumbered through the seas, rolling and pitching. The captain's wooden chest tipped and slid forward, his books and photos spilling onto the floor. Jolene bent to gather the pictures — one of a young woman whom she surmised was his wife, and another of two young children. She returned them to the chest, but a second wave tipped it on its side. A third one sent it spinning across the room. Em tucked her drawstring pouch carefully inside her drysuit.

"The waves seem to come in threes," said Jolene after some time. She imagined the dragon swooping left, right and left again before diving to the lake bottom.

Frederick found them sitting together when he came off his shift. Water sloshed into the captain's quarters as he forced the door shut behind him. "I've never seen the likes of it," he told them. "Not in all my years of sailing." He sank wearily into a chair. "There's waves out there that are twice as high as the ship — over forty feet — and the winds, they've got to be seventy miles per hour or more." The wind screeched at a higher pitch. "And it's starting to change direction, too," he added. "That'll make for some horrific cross seas."

"What are cross seas?" asked Michael, even though something in his voice told Jolene that he didn't want to know.

"That's when the wind and the water run opposite one other." Frederick did not tell them the result, but they could all guess.

A voice cackled through a long tube that jutted down into the captain's quarters and Frederick leapt to his feet. He put his ear to the tube, his eyes growing wide. "They've spotted a boat, port side." Michael, Jolene and Em followed him onto the deck, grasping the ship's steel railing and holding on for their lives. The blizzard raged around them, stealing their words and reducing all communication to hand gestures and signals. Michael pointed into the water where the ominous hull of a freighter wallowed upside down. A man's head bobbed to the surface, then another beside him. Pulling a life preserver from its hook, Frederick tossed it to the man. Beside Frederick, a sailor tore another from the wall and hurled it into the sea. Jolene watched the men grab for them. It would be impossible to attempt a rescue in these seas. She watched a life preserver rise and fall at the mercy of the waves, and shouted to the men. The wind silenced the words on her lips. A hand broke free of the surface then sank. It did not reappear. The life preserver was swept away.

Frederick gestured at them to return to the cabin, but as they tried to turn back, a wave hit the pilothouse, knocking out two windows and smashing the wooden door. The boat heeled sharply, threatening to tip. Jolene screamed and grabbed for the railing. She saw the wheelsman skid across the pilothouse. He pulled himself to his feet and gripped the wheel. The boat lurched into another trough, the storm knocking Jolene to her knees. She felt Frederick's strong arm around her and rose as the boat recovered. With slow, measured steps, the three of them and Frederick managed to return to the captain's quarters.

"I'm going up to the pilothouse," said Frederick after they had struggled to close the door against the violence of the storm. "You stay here and listen at the speaking tube. Do what the captain says, understand?" For a moment, he reminded Jolene of Grandpa. He pried the door open and ventured out into the elements. Jolene wondered if she would ever see him again.

"We're going to die, aren't we?" Em's eyes were blank.

Michael said nothing. Jolene made no response. The same thought had occurred to both of them.

Suddenly the boat surged forward. Jolene pressed her face against the ice-covered windows. Michael came to stand beside her. "I'm betting the *Regina* was lost with all hands," he said solemnly.

Jolene buried her face in his shoulder. Tears welled up in her eyes and her body trembled. They couldn't die like this. They weren't even supposed to be here. A voice hollered down the listening tube and Michael bounded towards it. "Anchor," he repeated. "They're anchoring the ship."

"Really?" asked Em. "Maybe we're close to shore." Jolene felt hope nudge her despair. She heard the muffled banging of machinery and Frederick burst through the door.

"We're taking on water," he told them. "The captain's going to anchor and save the power to run the pumps." He stroked his beard as if he couldn't believe what was happening. "Let's hope we're in close enough for the anchor to hit bottom." He raised his eyes towards the heavens and waited. Jolene felt the boat continue to heel. Then suddenly it steadied. Frederick did not move. "Hold," he breathed. "Hold." The *Regina* held. Frederick exhaled. "Now it's up to the pumps." He disappeared into the wind and weather.

Jolene, Michael and Em clung to the little hope Frederick had given them. If the pumps could keep the boat from flooding, they could ride out the storm safely anchored in water deep enough to keep them from being run aground on the rocks.

Together they waited, time weighing heavily on their hearts. The listening tube rumbled again and Jolene pressed her ear to it. The captain's words stopped her heart momentarily.

"What is it?" asked Michael.

In a daze, Jolene stepped away from the tube. "An order to abandon ship," she stated finally. The three of them stared at each other. The air in the suite grew thick with fear. Em whimpered and Michael trembled. Jolene reached beneath her dress collar and pulled the hood of her drysuit over her head, instructing Michael and Em to do the same.

"Let's go!" Frederick, his hair plastered against his head and his eyes crazed, was standing at the door. "We've lost power." With no further explanation, he handed them each a life jacket, which they pulled on and tied with nervous fingers. Frederick herded them onto the icy deck towards a lifeboat suspended over the side of the *Regina*. A sailor steadied the lifeboat and Michael climbed over the icy railing, followed by Em and Jolene. Frederick pressed a heavy coil of rope into Jolene's hands. "Lash yourselves to the boat," he thundered in her ear.

Jolene wound the rope around her waist, securing it with a bowline before passing it to Em and motioning for her to do the same. Em managed to do so as Jolene tried to tie the rope to the boat. The lifeboat lurched then plummeted as Frederick manned the pulleys. Jolene gripped its edges as Em handed Michael the remaining rope coil. If they could just wrap it around themselves and secure the ends. The boat dropped. Terror seized Jolene. Out of the darkness, a wave smashed the lifeboat into the steel hull of the *Regina*. Jolene heard the wood crack, felt the lifeboat teeter, then tip as the wave surged back from the boat. The freezing waters of Lake Huron engulfed them.

Chapter twenty-one

Adrenalin streamed through Jolene and she swam frantically for the surface, her dress dragging behind her. She broke through, catching sight of Em. A wave swept her under again and she fought her way back to the surface, the lights of the *Regina* reflecting off the water.

"Help!" screamed Em beside her, but the only reply was the frenetic churning of the lake. They were being carried away from the anchored *Regina*. Soon her lights were small pinpoints that the storm mercilessly extinguished. The steady blast of a whistle haunted the darkness — the *Regina's* final distress call.

Buoyed by her life jacket, Jolene turned away from the eerie sound and searched for Michael. The rope had held her and Em together, but the end of it stretched away like a long water snake. "Michael!" Jolene saw a sparkle behind her and turned just in time to be submerged by an enormous wave. She grabbed for Em and sank into the darkness, her lungs screaming with pain.

"Ahh!" Em was gasping for breath beside her. Jolene panted, then inhaled as another wave hit, shoving them down into the dragon's lair. Her lungs burned and threatened to burst. She struggled to the surface. Gasping, she drew piercing breaths. Beside her, Em hyperventilated and Jolene remembered that the waves came in threes. She squeezed Em's hand and took a deep breath as the third wave arrived. Her head throbbed and her lungs bellowed as they broke free of the dragon's grip once more.

"Michael!" Jolene cried as soon as she was able to. The rope lay limp in the water. She reached for it. "No! No!" Em's hands were beside hers, reeling in the rope, hand over hand. Suddenly it went taut. On the edge of the darkness, Jolene saw a rectangular shape. She reefed on the rope and her brother's face came into view. He was lying face down on what appeared to be a liferaft. "Michael!" Jolene and Em's voices pierced the wind, alerting the dragon to their presence once again.

A wave hit. Jolene held onto Em with one hand and the rope with the other. She counted the waves, surfacing after each one, her chest hammering with pain. Immediately after the third one had passed, she and Em began pulling the rope towards them. Soon, they were clutching the wooden planks of the liferaft. For a split second, Jolene wondered where it had come from — if yet another boat had been dragged under the stormy seas. Jolene shoved Em's body from below as Em hoisted herself onto the raft, kicking feverishly. Then she hauled herself aboard. Jolene let her head drop to the wooden planks. "Michael," she whispered touching his face. Her hand came away bloody, but she could feel his warm breath on her cheek.

The dragon roared and attacked again. Em clung to the planks and Jolene clung to the raft and Michael, riding out the creature's fury. At the first sign of a lull, Jolene re-secured the rope around her waist and looped it over a splintered plank. She wrapped it underneath Michael, who was still unconscious. The straps of his lifejacket had miraculously caught on the broken planks. Then she screamed at Em to do the same. By the time the next series of waves hit, they were lashed to the raft — at the mercy of the storm.

Despite her drysuit, Jolene grew chilled. Her fingers were stiff and the unprotected skin on her face began to tingle. She nudged Em. "Cover your face," she told her, stretching the neck of Michael's drysuit over his mouth and nose. She pulled the top of her own hood as far over her forehead as she could and adjusted her brother's until only his eyes were visible. She tucked her hands under her armpits.

A wall of water rose threateningly. If only they could see the waves coming, they could draw enough breath to ride them out. With empty lungs, the pain was unbearable. "Jo?"

Michael's voice called to her after an intense succession of waves.

"Michael," Jolene screamed. "Are you okay?"

He moaned. "I think I got knocked out after I found the raft, but I'm okay." His voice was exhausted and weak, but at least he was conscious.

They huddled together, lying first on their right sides and then on their left, calling each other's names as the storm drove their tiny raft through the darkness. Wave after wave after wave after wave. Fatigue weighed Jolene down. She struggled to shake it off, noticing that both Michael and Em seemed to be nodding off periodically. "At least one of us has to stay awake," said Jolene. "It's too dangerous otherwise. I'll go first."

"Wiggle your toes," advised Em sleepily. "It's impossible to fall asleep while you're wiggling your toes."

Jolene wiggled her toes as the waves and wind continued their assault. When she could no longer do so, she shook Em. Some time later, Michael woke his sister and so it continued. Ice encapsulated their clothing but they remained dry beneath their drysuits. The storm raged all through the night and into the morning. Jolene woke Em and dozed, her dream images riding the crest of each wind-whipped wave: Michael holding his salmon, Dad in his museum, Grandpa twirling his moustache, she and Michael fighting the dragon. The creature reared, its eagle's beak darting at them, its massive wings beating the air into a fury. But they did not retreat. She charged at it, brandishing hot rolls. Lion claws raked the air and Michael leapt onto the creature's back, sending it writhing and twisting into a fury.

"Jo." Michael's voice interrupted her sleep and Jolene raised her head. Between them, Em peered past frosted eyelashes. A heavy, thick snow had spread a clean quilt over the raft.

Em stared at the immaculate covering. "Are we dead?"

Her question made Jolene wonder if heaven were as white as snow. She brushed the flakes from her eyelashes. In no time, they were white again. She sank back onto the raft, her thoughts drifting towards the sky.

A thin light reflected off the snow the next time she opened her eyes. The winds still gusted and the flakes continued to fall. Jolene shook Em and Michael and they raised themselves, crinkling their icy covers. The grey-green waters seemed less tumultuous. Jolene searched the horizon. Which way had they been blown? Were they close to shore? Michael shifted stiffly on the raft and checked his watch. "It's ten-thirty-five a.m.," he told them.

As close as Jolene could figure, they'd been on the raft for more than sixteen hours. Sixteen hours after being shipwrecked, they were still alive. "Shipwreck survivors," murmured Michael. "It's got a nice ring to it."

"Now's the part where we drift up onto a sandy beach with lounge chairs and drinks with those little umbrellas," said Em.

Jolene's face was too cold to smile, but she was grateful for Em's relentless sense of humour and her brother's optimism. However, one look at them made her anxiety return. The bridge of Em's nose had a white patch on it and Michael looked pale and gaunt. She had to get them off the lake.

Em sucked on a clump of snow. "I want to go home," she said, mimicking an impatient toddler.

The raft floated. Words and phrases rose and fell with the swell of the waves. For hours they drifted, with no glimpse of land. Em knelt on the edge of the raft and leaned out towards the water, lifting a boot and an oar from the lake. She laid them on the raft, solemn reminders that others had not been as fortunate as they had. "I wonder what happened to Frank?" she asked the leaden sky.

The twins did not reply.

"And Frederick?" continued Em.

"I'm guessing it was his last trip, just as he said," said Jolene sadly.

"And Captain McCallum's," said Em.

"And the crew's and the cook's," added Michael.

The raft bobbed up and down. By mid-afternoon, the visibility was much better, but they still could not see the shoreline. "How big is this lake, anyway?" Michael sounded disgruntled.

"331 kilometres long and 294 kilometres wide," replied Em. "I had to memorize that once."

Jolene gazed upwards. Although she had been hoping the

sun would break through, the sky now seemed darker and the air felt heavier. Surely the storm had blown itself out by now. By late afternoon, she was not so certain. The snow resumed and the gusts blew again, making Jolene wonder who had accidentally roused the dragon.

Jolene's thoughts drifted. Michael was hurt and weak. Em was Em — passionate but not always practical. Jolene knew that if they were going to survive, it would be up to her. A fiery warmth filled her. They were going to survive! She could and she would find a way. Strength and determination rose within her, each wave confirming what she already knew. She had a clear, logical, ingenious mind. She was strong and healthy and she loved her brother with an intensity that defied words. He deserved to live, to laugh, to swim. And Em deserved to fight for women's rights and experience the love of a family. And she had a whole, wonderful, intense life ahead of her. Despite her weariness, Jolene felt awake and alive. There were mysteries in the world to solve and injustices in the world to be put right. Jolene's fingers tingled, but she didn't know if it was with excitement or the cold.

With reluctant resignation, Jolene acknowledged the need to stay warm and lay back down on the raft. Seconds felt like minutes, which seemed like hours, which felt like days. They nodded off, drifting between fantasy and reality. In her dream world, Jolene heard a horn blare. Awakened, she raised her head, seeing the faint outline of a vessel in the distance. She must be hallucinating. She rubbed her eyes, expecting the image to disappear. It remained — a large vessel bearing straight towards them.

"Michael! Em!" She raised herself on one arm. "It's a ship."

"A ship?" Em's voice was barely audible.

A horn sounded again and the girls scrambled to their knees. "Hello! Hello!" screamed Em, waving her arms.

"They can't hear us or see us," said Michael.

Jolene watched the boat's silhouette grow larger and larger. "It's headed right for us," she said, calculating its advance.

She grabbed the oar and dug its blade into the water, propelling them forward. Em wrenched a loose raft board free and frantically worked the other side. The ship's hull bore down on them, drawing closer and closer.

"The *Northern Queen*," read Em as the name of the ship became legible.

"Hurry!" hollered Jolene. "Faster."

Michael raised his head. "It's going to ram us!"

"We have to get past its centre line," panted Jolene.

The hull was metres away. Jolene dug the paddle into the water with all her strength as a huge swell running off the side of the boat caught the raft and sent it spinning diagonally. The children clutched the boards, abandoning their efforts to paddle. Gradually, the raft began to dip and rise again. Jolene lifted her head. The image of the boat receded in the wind-blown snow. Behind them, they heard a crunch as the *Northern Queen* ran aground on a sandbar.

"Do you think she'll break up?" asked Michael, holding onto the raft and looking back over his shoulder.

"I don't know." Jolene's back ached and a pain pulsed from her shoulder to her neck. "But we have to be close to shore if she ran aground." She peered into the growing darkness. "Look! Rocks!" A jagged outcropping jutted out into the lake. Jolene could just make out the outline of the shore.

"Paddle," yelled Em, picking up the oar. But the raft was caught in a fast current and no amount of paddling could alter its course. "It's no use."

"Be patient," counselled Jolene. "It's a lake. Eventually, we have to run into land."

But night eroded even Jolene's patience. Michael and Em curled up and slept, but Jolene remained sitting on the raft, wondering where they were, which direction they were being blown in. Dad had mentioned that most of the wreckage had ended up south of Goderich on the Canadian shore. On and on they drifted. The wind had lessened and pinpricks of stars were visible above her. She glanced towards shore, her eyes drawn to a faint glow in the distance. She watched it, the point of light a steady beacon of hope.

Carefully, so as not to rouse the others with false hopes, Jolene held the oar by its handle and dipped it in the water. She could not touch bottom, but the beacon of light was growing brighter and the water calmer. Again, she tried to measure the depth of the water. This time her oar bumped against something before floating freely. The raft sailed onwards, but Jolene had the distinct impression that they were moving more slowly. The light appeared to be expanding from a point to a square.

Jolene began to paddle. The light was coming closer. "What's going on?" murmured Michael's voice.

"I can see a light, but I'm afraid that we're going to sail past it."

Her brother tried to sit up but collapsed back onto the raft. Jolene paddled with a strength she didn't know she possessed.

Em struggled to her knees. "I can see the shore," she said suddenly. "There's a point ahead." Jolene dug the paddle deep, catching as much water as possible with the blade. The land came closer and closer and Jolene's oar struck bottom. Em leapt from the raft and Jolene followed, splashing through the knee-deep water and hauling the raft to shore behind them. Groping her way onto the beach below the square of light, Jolene felt her boots sink into the sand and the odd sensation that came with being on solid land again. She let the rope fall and sank gratefully to the ground.

Chapter twenty-two

Em was on her knees beside Jolene. "Land!" She bent forward to kiss it, returning upright with snow stuck to her lips.

The girls removed their life jackets and helped Michael from the raft. He was dizzy and weak, but tried valiantly to stand. "Now what?" asked Em, looking about.

The wind howled and Jolene lowered her voice, so as not to aggravate the wary dragon. "There's something up on that hill," she said, gesturing at the beacon of light above them. "Come on." They stumbled forward through the snow, across rocks and driftwood strewn with wreckage.

"Ouch!" Em bent to retrieve the obstacle she had tripped

over and Michael staggered. She caught him before he fell. "It's a bottle of something."

"Leave it be," advised Jolene, but Em tucked it under her arm.

By the time they'd reached the base of the hill, Em had found three bottles of something. Slowly they navigated a trail through the snow and debris. A small barn stood atop the hill, its only illuminated window the beacon Jolene had seen from the raft. She wondered if somebody had intentionally left it burning.

Inching the barn door open, the children stepped inside. Warm, musty air assaulted their noses and they heard the agitated hooves of the animals reacting to their presence. Michael sat down on a hay bale. Em put the bottles down and pulled the lit lantern from its hook.

She waved the light about, revealing five dairy cows and two workhorses in stalls on their right. Opposite the stalls, a mound of sweet-smelling hay stood beside a tack room. The horses stamped their feet and the cows lowed softly. "Hay makes a great bed," advised Em, making Jolene wonder how she knew. "We can hang our clothes over the stalls to dry." Em removed her dress and stood in the barn's warmth in her drysuit. Jolene also disrobed and helped Michael do the same. She tore a piece of cloth from her hem and dabbed at the wound on his forehead. Thankfully, it was not too deep. Finally, they waded into the haystack.

Snuggled into the itchy hay, Jolene was glad that her drysuit was full length. She felt the tremendous weight of her eyelids and was only vaguely aware of the horses shuffling as she was pulled into the thick fleece of sleep.

The gentle lowing of cows grew more persistent. Jolene woke first, inhaling the rich, pungent smell of fresh manure. The horror of the night had given way to the first soft rays of dawn and hope. She pushed a path out of the haystack and brushed her drysuit clean. The cows mooed more loudly, demanding to be milked. "Michael! Em! Wake up!" She shook her brother as Em sat upright, hay protruding in every direction from her hair.

Michael looked much improved and stronger after his rest. His stomach growled and Jolene smiled. If he was hungry, that was a good sign. They dressed as daylight peeked through the window of the barn. Em squatted beside the door and examined the bottles she had found on the beach. "Whiskey," she declared picking up the first one. "And more whiskey." She lifted the last glass jar. "And peaches!"

The mere mention of food made the children salivate. "Let's get out of here first. Then we'll eat and figure out what to do." Jolene slid the barn door open and stepped into the snow-lit day.

A small cove lay below them, drifts of snow littered with wood, articles of clothing and debris. Jolene shuddered. Those were the wreckage of boats and the belongings of sailors who had been caught in the storm. She tried to remember how many sailors had been killed, then tried to forget.

They traipsed down the hill and settled on a large piece of driftwood, breaking the seal of the jar and hungrily devouring the canned peaches. "I'm starving," said Michael, speaking for all of them. "I wonder if any more food's come ashore."

"Forget the food," insisted Jolene. "We need to find a time crease and get back to the present. Gramps will be worried sick." She surveyed the cove. Grandpa had told Em that there would be time creases all along Lake Huron. But neither she nor Michael had ever actually discovered one before.

"What would we look for?" asked Em, eyeing the sun, which had barely risen above the horizon. "A shadow?"

"A hot shadow," said Michael.

"Right!" declared Em, dubiously. She remained seated on the driftwood.

Jolene refused to let desperation overcome her. There had to be a way back to the present. A movement caught her eye and she jumped up from her seat. An older boy was combing the beach near the water's edge, collecting things. Jolene rushed towards him, her feet kicking a metal object beneath the snow. She bent to retrieve it — a pocket watch with a silver chain.

"Hey you! Leave off!" The boy ran towards her, shaking his fist in the air. Jolene stood her ground as he advanced, a sneer on his face. "That's mine!" he said, wrenching the watch from Jolene's hands and summoning Michael and Em to her side. Jolene could smell alcohol on the boy's breath.

He planted his feet firmly, squared his broad shoulders and stared defiantly at the children. He was much taller and stronger than them and malice emanated from him. "Go find yourselves another beach to loot," he snarled. "Bright's Grove is mine."

Bright's Grove! Jolene had awakened at Bright's Grove the morning they had driven to Sarnia. That meant they were on the Canadian side of Lake Huron about ten minutes drive from the Sarnia marina in the present. She guessed that translated to about ten kilometres and felt a flutter of excitement inside her. If they could just reach Sarnia, she knew where the time crease at the marina was located.

"Come on," said Em. "We're not looking for trouble." She pulled on Jolene's dress sleeve, but Jolene did not move. A plan was taking shape in her head.

"What did you find?" she asked the boy, ignoring Em's tug.

The boy dug into his pocket and proudly displayed a gold locket and a man's wallet. Jolene wondered whose they had been and where those people were now. "Is that all?" she scoffed, turning to leave.

The boy's hand gripped her shoulder. "What have you got?"

Jolene shrugged. "Stuff. Good stuff, but not what we're looking for." She pivoted slowly on her heel.

"What are you looking for?" demanded the boy.

"A ride to Sarnia."

"My brother's going to Sarnia this morning. He plays for their hockey team and was supposed to report for the season Sunday." Jolene wondered what day it was. "I might be able to arrange something." He leaned forward with a menacing scowl. "What you got?"

"Two bottles of whiskey!" Jolene heard Em gulp.

Desire flared in the boy's eyes. He looked past her at the snow-covered beach. "It's a deal," he said quietly. "The whiskey first!"

"Where do you live?" asked Jolene.

The boy pointed to a rooftop half-hidden by trees.

"Let's go. We'll bring the bottles," she promised. Michael and Em scampered back to their driftwood bench and returned with the whiskey while the boy returned to his collection, wrapping it in a canvas cloth.

"He's not even old enough to drink," whispered Michael.

"But he's dumb enough to," added Em. She flashed the boy an artificial smile and followed him towards the house. Lake Huron had grown calmer. The dragon still huffed and snorted in the distance, but it appeared to be returning to its watery lair.

Once they had reached the house, the boy stopped. "Hand it over!"

Jolene proffered the bottles and the greedy boy disappeared into the barn. He returned with his brother and within minutes, the children had fabricated a plausible story about becoming separated from their grandfather in the storm. They were informed that the horses were just being hitched to the sleigh.

When the sleigh was ready, they clambered aboard, snuggling under the blankets in the back. The horses set out at a slow, even walk, picking their way down the snowy roads. Jolene settled in between Em and Michael for the journey to Sarnia. Within minutes, the rhythmic gait of the horses had lulled them all to sleep.

It was early afternoon by the time they reached the harbour at Sarnia, which was teeming with sailors, men and women anxiously awaiting and dreading news. The telegraph lines had been down and the full extent of the storm's toll was only just becoming known as tugs and rescue vehicles ventured onto the lakes and the bodies of the storm's victims began to wash ashore.

The children hurried to the shed where they had originally time-travelled in Sarnia, trying to block out the tragedy and morbid speculation that surrounded them. Slipping behind the battered building, Jolene felt the dense, warm air that marked the time crease. "One location in time," she murmured, squeezing Em's hand, and feeling the air pressure increase and her body stretch. Jolene closed her eyes, the weight of the air crushing her chest. Then suddenly, her body was thrown forward.

Chapter twenty-three

When Jolene opened her eyes, she was standing at the lifeguard station in the sunny present. She threw an arm around Michael and another around Em. Michael's dimples dotted his cheeks. Em's auburn hair blew wildly in the warm summer breeze. "Now what?" she asked.

"Let's get out of these clothes," suggested Jolene.

"Good idea," agreed Em. "We're at the marina so our dry-suits won't look too conspicuous."

They changed in the nearby public washrooms, rolled their clothes into bundles and decided to go barefoot. "Where do you think Gramps is?" asked Michael.

"Just a phone call away, if we had any money." Jolene

stared at the bulge around Em's neck. "Do you still have your cell phone, Em?"

Jolene could see Em's eyes dilate like a cat's. "I tucked it inside my drysuit." She reached inside her suit and unlooped the drawstring pouch from her neck. Her fingers pulled the phone from the pouch. "It's dry, but I haven't used it for months."

Michael punched the power button. A red light glowed and the phone sang. Em bounced up and down on the spot. "Did you have an account?" asked Jolene.

"It wasn't mine," Em reminded her.

Jolene took the phone from Em's hand and dialled the numbers of the cell phone in the RV. The three of them bent over the silver rectangle. It beeped, lapsed into silence, then rang. Em's feet drummed against the pier beneath her. The phone rang a second time. Jolene gripped the receiver tighter, willing someone to answer.

"Hello." Grandpa's voice was clear and anxious.

"Gramps," Jolene breathed into the receiver. "Gramps, it's Jo."

It took Grandpa less than fifteen minutes to reach them. He had been out looking for them in the vicinity where the debris from the Regina had washed ashore after the storm. As the RV came to a stop, the children started towards it. Grandpa hurried towards them, sweeping the three of them into his arms and crushing them in his embrace. "You're here! You're safe!" Tears glistened on his cheeks. He steered them towards the RV, herding them up the stairs. Chaos rubbed against Jolene's leg. She scooped him up and snuggled him close, but the rubbery feel of the drysuits repulsed him.

"Thank goodness you were wearing those suits," said Grandpa. None of them wanted to think about what would have happened if they had not been.

Grandpa cleaned Michael's head wound and then, satisfied that they were otherwise unharmed, took charge. He drove to a nearby park, hung their drysuits and clothes on tree branches and ordered them to change while he made soup and grilled cheese sandwiches with an energy that surprised them all. "I didn't know what to do after you sailed off," he told them. "I thought about calling the police, but I was pretty certain they'd have locked me up with a story like mine." He placed the ketchup on the table. "And I didn't know what I was going to tell your parents. Your dad left his cell phone in the RV, so I couldn't reach him anyway. It's probably just as well. Your mom phoned once, but I wasn't in." He tucked a curl behind Jolene's ear. "I spent all my time reading every detail I could about the storm and combing the beaches, hoping that by some miracle, you'd come ashore alive."

Grandpa served up lunch and Chaos scampered across the children's laps trying to get closer to the cheese. "I'm starved," said Michael, reaching for a sandwich.

"What day is it?" asked Jolene.

"Tuesday afternoon," Grandpa answered. "You set sail Sunday." In just three days, he had lost weight, and deep black depressions ringed his eyes. A hollow gauntness sunk his cheeks behind his moustache. Jolene bit into her sandwich, aware that grilled cheese had never tasted so good.

The kettle sang and Grandpa soon had four hot chocolates on the table; he then added a squirt of whipping cream to each one. Chaos immediately stuck his nose in Michael's, then happily licked off the cream.

They laughed and Jolene was overcome by the warmth and safety of the moment. "It's so good to have you back," said Grandpa. "All I could think about was the three of you in the middle of that storm, with those sub-freezing temperatures, hurricane winds and that blinding blizzard." He closed his eyes against the images. Nobody responded. There would be time enough for those stories later.

Michael reached for his fourth sandwich and Em and Jolene for their third each. When they had eaten their fill, Grandpa cleaned up and announced that he would drive to Goderich. Michael yawned, stretching out on the couch. His head dropped to his chest before they had pulled out of the parking lot. Em, still seated at the kitchen table, had already nodded off. Climbing into her loft bed with Chaos, Jolene was aware of sleep weighing down her body and mind. She tried to wiggle her toes, but it was too late.

Sunshine danced on the covers of her bed. Jolene blinked herself awake and looked out at the familiar scenery of the

RV resort in Goderich. Grandpa was at the sink, preparing a snack. "Your dad is due back in Goderich tonight." Jolene descended from the loft, put an arm around his back and let her head rest on his shoulder. He kissed her forehead and smiled. Chaos let out a loud, jealous meow, waking both Em and Michael.

Grandpa set some cookies and fruit out on the table and the children ate again, as if they had not eaten just two hours earlier. Grandpa joined them, holding his coffee mug and biding his time to make an important announcement. "After everything that's happened today," he said choosing a silent moment, "we are through time travelling. All of us."

"But I need to go back," insisted Em.

"Why?" asked Michael.

"For Mary, William, George and Celeste," answered Jolene.

"Exactly," said Em. Her blue eyes regarded Grandpa from beneath her long eyelashes. "John and Edward were on the *Wexford*," she began. "Did they . . ."

Grandpa responded to the unfinished question. "Some of the boats on Lake Huron were stranded and their crews saved. Unfortunately, the *Wexford* wasn't one of them. Like the *Regina*, she was caught in the open waters. She sank fourteen kilometres from shore, taking her entire crew with her."

Jolene squeezed Em's hand. Tears filled her friend's lower eyelids but did not fall.

Grandpa went on. "Historians believe that the *Wexford*

reached Goderich mid-afternoon on Sunday, but the conditions made it too difficult to enter the harbour." Jolene recalled what the harbour master had told them about the breakwaters, foghorn and lighthouse. "Some of the residents thought they heard distress whistles. It's likely that she tried to come ashore south of Goderich. The shipwreck was found a few years ago, not far from here." He traced the rim of his cup with his index finger. "I'm sorry, Em, but I can tell you this." Em looked up, a single tear like a raindrop on her cheek. "When they discovered the shipwreck of the *Wexford,* it was obvious that the crew had tried to launch some lifeboats before she sunk."

Jolene envisioned John and Edward, determined to reach their loved ones, launching a boat in the storm. Perhaps that experience had been similar to their own launch from the *Regina.* Without drysuits, the men would have died of hypothermia, but the fact that they might have tried to reach shore made her feel better.

"What happened to the *Northern Queen?*" asked Jolene.

"She was one of the lucky ones. She ran aground but managed to launch two lifeboats and save her crew before the ship broke up," answered Grandpa. "Why do you ask?"

Jolene recalled the frightening presence of the boat steaming towards them. "Just curious," she replied, unwilling to speak yet about the fear and tragedy that had made the last three days unforgettable ones.

"The storm brought one tragedy after another." Grandpa

sipped his coffee. "One of the boats, the *Price,* capsized in the middle of Lake Huron. Shortly after the storm subsided, sailors reported seeing the upside down hull of a large freighter in the lake." Jolene stopped chewing. They had seen the same. "Days later a diver identified it as the *Price.* Nobody survived, except the assistant engineer." All three children looked up. "He walked off the ship before she sailed. Said he had a premonition about the trip."

"I wish the engineer on the *Regina* had walked off the ship," said Em. "I never got to meet Frank."

"I'm sorry," repeated Grandpa. "You can't change history. Which is why," he continued, "I will not allow any of you to return to 1913 again."

"But I have to!" declared Em.

"No!" Grandpa was on his feet. "You belong here, Em, just like Jolene and Michael." His gaze was as fiery as Jolene had ever seen. "This afternoon, when Doug returns, we will contact the proper authorities and return you to your home."

Em was on her feet. "No! I refuse . . ."

"Enough!" Grandpa's voice silenced her. He turned his back on them, exiting the RV with his articles and books.

"He can't do that!" protested Em. "I'm going back, no matter what."

Jolene reached for her friend's hand. "I know," she said softly. "Just be patient."

Within an hour, Grandpa was sound asleep on the lounge

chair outside the RV. The girls fetched their clothing and changed quickly. "Cover for us, won't you Michael?" Jolene whispered. An uncomfortable look passed over her face. "Gramps always said that I'd know when I found the thing in life that I really wanted to do. If he knew Em better, he'd understand that this is what she has to do right now." Michael nodded and the two girls slipped through the hedge.

As they approached the time crease, Jolene reached for Em's hand, but she pulled it away. She needed to know she could time travel on her own. They stepped into the hot shadows, allowing time to pass by them until Goderich, 1913, battered and beaten, surrounded them. A cool wind left over from the storm blew and the harbour buzzed with activity. Fishing boats and tugs bobbed up and down on the rough waters off shore. Jolene guessed they were searching for survivors. She knew they'd find only bodies.

Em and Jolene filed up the hill, wrapping their silence tightly around them. George met them at the top of the escarpment. "You're safe!" he cried, throwing his arms around Em and embracing Jolene as well.

Em withdrew from his hug. "We've heard news about the *Wexford*."

Hope glimmered faintly in George's eyes. "Were there any survivors?"

"None." Em's voice fluttered on the wind. It was such a small word and yet so huge.

"They found life preservers and bodies south of here," Jolene said gently.

George clenched his fists against the pain. "I expected as much." He turned his back on the lake. Together, they walked to Wellington Street. While George and Em went inside, Jolene sat on the front porch, feeling only emptiness and pain. George came out first and sat beside Jolene. He handed her an envelope. "This is for you," he said. Jolene withdrew a picture of herself and Em, heads bowed together, faces filled with joyous laughter.

"Thanks," she told George as the door opened and a sad Em reappeared.

"Celeste's gone to the post office to check the lists of the dead," she said. "I'm going to find her."

Jolene stood. "Want some company?"

"Yes!" said Em simply. "Please."

The two girls trudged through the snow. Billboards lay in pieces and broken tree branches littered the streets. Snow was piled high on both sides of the road.

As they approached the post office, Jolene caught sight of Celeste in the throng of people outside. They were all waiting for news, and for almost all of them, the news would be devastating. Em stopped and Jolene could feel her distress. "I'll come back one day, Jo. Just not now."

Jolene placed a hand on Em's shoulder. "I know, Em."

Without warning, Em threw her arms around Jolene. Then she turned towards the anxious faces in the crowd and clenched her jaw. "I'd better go find Celeste." She hesitated. "Do you think she's forgiven me for all the awful things I said?" Jolene nodded resolutely. "I wish I was more like you,"

Em said unexpectedly. "I'm too pushy and opinionated." She turned away and manoeuvred her way through those gathered.

Jolene watched as Em reached Celeste, was greeted with an excited embrace, and then pulled her sister aside. At that point, Jolene turned away. The pain was too raw and sharp. Celeste had lost her fiancé. She and George had lost a brother. Mary and William had lost a son. And these people gathered together had lost husbands, sons, fathers, nephews, cousins and friends. Jolene looked up at the stoic faces of the old stone buildings on the opposite side of the street. She could do nothing to change history, but the cruelty of it tore at her heart. She looked helplessly in the direction of Lake Huron.

Jolene accompanied Em and a sobbing Celeste home, feeling numb as she watched Mary embrace her daughter. In a stupor, she heard Em tell them that Frank's life had been taken before she had met him. Jolene stood robot-like at the front door as Mary and Celeste embraced Em, feeling her pain despite their own grief. They would help each other survive this terrible tragedy. Jolene slipped quietly away, back towards the harbour and through the time crease one last time.

Chapter twenty-four

Back in the twenty-first century, Jolene elected to climb the hill into town before returning to the RV. There was something she had to do, something she had to check into. After a stop at the library, she made her way across Courthouse Square, lingering for a moment at the notice board. The poster depicting the diver was still there and Jolene felt herself drawn to it. She had liked the sensation of diving from the pool edge, but springboard diving also involved the aerial twists and turns she had loved in gymnastics. She felt her heart skip a beat and a sudden surge of warmth within her. The air smelled of approaching rain as Jolene reached the RV, bracing herself for her grandfather's anger.

Grandpa looked up as she entered. "Where were you?"

"At the library," replied Jolene. It wasn't exactly a lie.

"Em went back to 1913?"

"Yes," said Jolene. "At least for now."

Grandpa looked pensive. "Well, I suppose that ultimately it was her decision to make," he admitted reluctantly.

Jolene sighed in relief. She had hoped that he might come to see the wisdom of his own advice and he had. Depositing the envelope on the table, she withdrew a photocopied picture of two young women embracing one another. "Come and look at this," she told Michael and Grandpa.

They joined her, studying the image of the two women. One was obviously Em, slightly older and with short, stylish hair. The other was undoubtedly a radiant Celeste. Michael read the caption aloud. "Dr. Celeste Gordon and Miss Em Brighton raise their voices during a suffragette rally."

Celeste had become a doctor and married. Em had become a suffragette and made a difference.

Jolene extracted the photo George had given her from the envelope and showed her brother. "Now that's a great memory," said Michael.

The phone rang and Dad announced that they had just docked at Goderich. He was bubbling over with excitement when they picked him up. "The best wrecks were the *Wexford* and the *Regina*," he said. "The *Wexford's* sitting upright and the *Regina's* anchor still holds. But the strangest thing was that bodies from another boat, the *Price,* washed ashore wearing life preservers from the *Regina*. Amazing!" Jolene and Michael exchanged sad smiles but said nothing.

"Who knows what heroes sailed the lakes that night," said Grandpa. Jolene thought of Frederick lowering their lifeboat. There had likely been many acts of heroism the night of the Great Storm, but many of them had been in vain.

"They still haven't found some of the shipwrecks," Dad informed them. "One of the missing wrecks was a huge freighter that sank on her maiden voyage."

"Like the *Griffon*," said Michael, catching his sister's eye.

"It must have been awful in Goderich after the storm," commented Dad.

"It was," remembered Jolene.

"They held a big funeral procession and the whole town turned out for the ceremony. Five unidentified sailors were buried in the Goderich cemetery and they still mark the event with an annual mariners' church service." Grandpa's voice faded.

"Nineteen ships went to the bottom of the Great Lakes," said Dad. "Nineteen others were stranded or beached and 244 sailors were killed."

"The *Wexford* might have survived if the Goderich harbour had been like it is today," said Jolene.

"Maybe," agreed Grandpa.

"And perhaps the *Regina* would have made it if she'd run aground," said Michael.

"Maybe," said Grandpa. "Those who survived the storm said they'd never seen anything like it before. And experts agree that it was the greatest storm ever to hit the Great Lakes in recorded history."

Jolene looked out at the glistening waters of Lake Huron. There were some things that even the most passionate desire could not overcome.

Dad pushed Michael's hair back from his forehead, revealing the bandage that covered his scratch. "What happened?" he asked

"Something ran into me," replied Michael. He quickly changed the subject. "I'm going to the pool for a workout."

"Hang on," said Jolene. "I'm coming."

The others looked at her like she was crazy. "The dive club meets tonight," she explained. "I want to watch them."

"Okay," agreed Dad, smiling broadly. "Let me know what you think."

"I didn't know you liked diving," said Michael as they rode away.

"Neither did I," admitted Jolene. When she had seen the poster a week ago, the diver had only reminded her of the past. Now, the image of the twisting diver seemed to hold an exciting connection to her future. "I think it would be neat to dive from those high boards."

"Not me!" said Michael, referring to his fear of heights. "I wouldn't come off one of those high diving boards if you paid me."

Jolene grinned at him. They were twins, but they were definitely individuals.

By the time the dive club had finished for the day, Jolene had decided that diving was something she would like to look into back in Calgary. She glided down the hill with her brother, feeling tired but content. It was still early when she climbed into her loft bed. As her eyes closed, her dream highway emerged.

The highway, like the tail of a fat grey lizard, stretches before Jolene. Waves of heat dance above the hot asphalt. Confidently, she places one foot in front of the other, following the solid, white centre line. Far ahead, on the horizon, the line and road merge. Jolene slows. She glances over her shoulder, searching for her twin brother, Michael, her father, mother and grandfather, but they are absent. The road belongs to her alone and that is exhilarating. Smiling, Jolene resumes walking. She peers at the horizon. Is that her destination? One of many destinations. Does she have the strength to reach it? If she cares about reaching it, passion, strength and determination will be hers. Excitement and anticipation fill her. The possibilities for the future swirl like clouds around her.

ABOUT THE AUTHOR

Cathy Beveridge was born and raised in Calgary and spent four years abroad in the Middle East. While there, she developed a keen interest in writing about Canada and upon her return wrote *Shadows of Disaster,* her first time-travel adventure, which brings to life Frank Slide, Canada's deadliest rockslide. *Shadows of Disaster* has been nominated for the Rocky Mountain Book Award, the Diamond Willow Award and the Red Cedar Book Award. This was followed by her second historical adventure, *Chaos in Halifax,* where Jolene and her twin brother find themselves trapped in the devastation of the Halifax explosion. Other publications include two contemporary young-adult novels, *Offside* (Thistledown, 2001), winner of the 2003 Saskatchewan Snow Willow Award, and *One on One* (Thistledown, 2005). Some of Cathy's short stories may be found in anthologies such as *Beginnings: Stories of Canada's Past* (Ronsdale, 2001) and *Up All Night* (Thistledown, 2001). Background information for the novel is available at www.ronsdalepress.com under *Stormstruck.*